This Book Belongs to Mrs. Sherry

THE
SALAMANDER
Spell

Books by E. D. Baker

THE TALES OF THE FROG PRINCESS:

THE FROG PRINCESS

DRAGON'S BREATH

ONCE UPON A CURSE

NO PLACE FOR MAGIC

THE SALAMANDER SPELL

THE
SALAMANDER
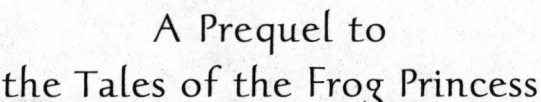

A Prequel to
the Tales of the Frog Princess

E. D. BAKER

SCHOLASTIC INC.
New York Toronto London Auckland Sydney
Mexico City New Delhi Hong Kong Buenos Aires

ISBN-13: 978-0-545-17483-1
ISBN-10: 0-545-17483-X

12 11 10 9 8 7 6 5 4 3 2 1   9 10 11 12 13 14/0

Printed in China   40

First Scholastic printing, October 2009

This book is dedicated to Ellie for being my first reader; to Kimmy, Nate, Emiko, Sophie, and Andy for their love and support; to Victoria for her insight; and to all my wonderful fans for being so encouraging.

One

Like everyone else, Grassina knew exactly how important the Green Witch was to Greater Greensward. Not only did the Green Witch have to defend the kingdom from invaders, whether magical or mundane, she also had to ensure that everything was in good working order, like the roads, the moat, and the castle itself. It was a full-time job, made doubly hard when she had royal duties as well.

Grassina's mother, Queen Olivene, had been the Green Witch since before her daughters were born. Although the queen wasn't very old, everyone knew that someday, someone would have to replace her. Since the title usually passed from mother to daughter, the whole kingdom had been watching Grassina's older sister, Chartreuse, for some sign that she had inherited her mother's talent for magic. Unfortunately, that sign had yet to show itself, and everyone was getting tired of waiting, especially thirteen-year-old Grassina.

Grassina set her hand on one of the thistles that grew at the edge of the moat and jerked it back, scowling. It wasn't fair. Chartreuse always got whatever she wanted—a horde of suitors, lessons in magic, a new kitten... Grassina, on the other hand, had to make do with her leftovers, just because she was the younger sister. Even her instructor in deportment, Lady Sophronia, had taught Chartreuse first, something the old woman mentioned daily. Whereas Chartreuse had been a prize pupil, Grassina was sadly lacking. Her curtsies were either too deep or not deep enough. Chartreuse's had been exactly right. Grassina's small talk wasn't witty. Chartreuse knew how to captivate everyone in the room. Grassina had yet to master the air of command that Lady Sophronia insisted all princesses must have. Everyone from scullery maids to the greatest noblemen paid attention to Chartreuse. Grassina's ineptness with her lessons didn't bother her at all; although she loved to learn, she didn't think anything Sophronia had to say was important enough to worry about. Chartreuse, of course, had considered her own deportment lessons vital.

Grassina was sure that even if Chartreuse hadn't mastered the art of courtly behavior, she would have been the court favorite. While Grassina hated her carrot red hair and too many freckles, Chartreuse was always tossing her honey gold curls and admiring her creamy complexion in the mirror. No matter what Chartreuse did, she was always pretty. She even looked good when she cried, because it made her blue eyes dewy so that she seemed sweet and vulnerable. All crying did to Grassina was turn her face red and splotchy.

Wiping a drop of blood from her pricked finger, she sat back on her heels, waiting impatiently for her sister to finish her lesson. Grassina had been kneeling beside the moat for so long that her legs were getting numb. That morning she'd overheard her mother telling Chartreuse where they would meet for their daily magic lesson, giving Grassina just enough time to look for a hiding place. The pile of stone blocks left over from repairing the tower was only a few yards from the edge of the moat, close enough to listen in on the conversation. It hid her if she stayed put, but wasn't big enough to conceal her if she moved more than a foot in either direction. Grassina shifted her weight ever so carefully, trying not to make a sound. Leaving before the lesson ended was out of the question since she wasn't supposed to be there in the first place and her mother was bound to see her if she stood up.

A medium-sized fish chased a school of minnows just below the smooth surface of the moat. Queen Olivene sighed and shook her head, turning to her older daughter. "You need to sound more confident when you recite a spell, Chartreuse. Listen closely. I'll do it again so you can hear what I mean. It's very simple, really. Just trace the letters in the water with your finger and say,

> Bubbles small and bubbles large,
> Put yourselves within my charge.
> On the water, write my name.
> 'Round it set a lovely frame.

Bubbles formed, gathering on the surface of the water until the name *Olivene* became legible and a circle of bubbles surrounded the word. The queen's name floated in place until a curious gray green fish rose to the surface and tried to bite one of the larger bubbles. The bubble burst with a loud *pop*, scaring the fish away. Grassina giggled, then clapped her hand over her mouth to stifle the sound. Chartreuse turned around and glanced in her direction, wearing a haughty look of disdain, which might have been more intimidating if Grassina hadn't caught her practicing that very same expression in a mirror that morning.

Knowing that there was no use hiding any longer, Grassina sighed and stood up. Queen Olivene frowned at her younger daughter. "Did you skip your lesson in deportment again? I'm sure Lady Sophronia is looking everywhere for you."

"I finished my lesson," said Grassina, her legs prickling as she shifted from one foot to the other.

"You're always poking your nose into things that don't

concern you," said Chartreuse. "It isn't as if you're going to get any magic. For two hundred years the firstborn daughter in our family has been the Green Witch. As the eldest . . ."

"I can't help it if I'm curious," said Grassina. "I love watching you do magic, Mother."

"It's your sister's turn now," said Olivene, and she turned back to Chartreuse. "I want you to try it again, but this time you have to show me that you believe in what you're doing."

"That's just it," said Chartreuse. "How can I believe it will work when it never has before?"

"It will in due time," said Olivene. "My grandmother didn't come into her magic until she was seventeen."

"So you've told me," muttered Chartreuse, her lips pursing into a pout. Dipping her finger in the water, Chartreuse wrote her name while repeating the spell in a more commanding tone. When nothing happened, she sighed and turned to her mother. "Tell me again what Father said about your magic when you first met."

A slow smile lit Olivene's face. "He told me that even without my magic, I was the most fascinating woman he'd ever met, but with my magic I was irresistible. I don't know how many times he said that he was honored that my parents had chosen him."

Chartreuse sighed. "That's so sweet. When I get married, it will be to a man who feels that way about me. He's going to love me to distraction and put me above every-thing else. He'll bring me gifts and take me to tourna-ments and write poems about my beauty just like Father did for you."

"That was a long time ago and we were both young," said Olivene. "Most husbands aren't so attentive."

"Mine will be," said Chartreuse. "I'm going to marry for love. Maybe Torrance or Limelyn. They're both very handsome."

For the last few months, one prince after another had come to visit from various kingdoms, hoping to win Chartreuse's hand in marriage. She had enjoyed all the at-tention and had been delighted when some of her more serious suitors decided to remain at the castle until she made up her mind.

"A handsome face isn't all you should be looking for," said Olivene.

"I know that. They have other good qualities, too. Torrance writes songs about me. He has the most won-derful singing voice, and his eyes . . . Have you noticed what a lovely shade of blue they are? Some of my friends fancy themselves in love with him. I think I might be, too. He says he'll have another song for me tonight."

"Prince Torrance comes from a good kingdom," said Queen Olivene. "But he wouldn't be your best choice. He's a second son, and his elder brother is reputed to be exceedingly healthy."

"There's also Limelyn," said Chartreuse. "He's terribly brave and has the nicest smile. I feel tingly when he kisses my hand."

Grassina stood up and stretched. "Have you noticed that she doesn't care if either of them has a brain or is honest or true? The man I marry must have a good heart and love me for myself. He must be smart and caring and—"

"No one asked for your opinion, pipsqueak," said Chartreuse.

Queen Olivene didn't look happy. "Limelyn is also a second son. His kingdom is small and poor. He wouldn't bring enough to the marriage to make it worth your while."

Chartreuse extended her hand over the water. "I'm going to try that spell again. Maybe if I concentrate harder . . ."

"Careful," said Grassina. "You'll give yourself a headache."

Chartreuse smiled sweetly at her sister. "Be nice, Grassina, and maybe I'll let you marry one of the other princes. Not Stephen or Clarence; they're both too serious, and I've never seen either one smile. Miguel, perhaps. You like animals and such, so you won't mind that he doesn't talk about anything except horses and dogs. I think he's a tremendous bore. I'm sure you'd find him fascinating."

"You're too kind," Grassina said.

7

"Or perhaps you'd prefer Rinaldo. He acts more like a merchant than a prince, but some people might think that's endearing. Princesses should never lie, Grassina, so be honest. Don't you think one of them would be ideal for you?"

Olivene looked annoyed. "Don't be so quick to dismiss them, Chartreuse. Miguel and Rinaldo may not share your interests, but they are both the sole heirs to sizeable kingdoms. Either one would be a good choice."

"Not for me, Mother," said Chartreuse. "All either one cares about is his own kingdom. I want a husband who will care about Greater Greensward. Now be quiet, Grassina, so I can try this spell again."

Grassina held her breath as her sister recited the simple poem. Chartreuse had tried one spell after another over the last few years, but so far not one of them had worked. Part of Grassina wanted her sister to succeed. After all, the kingdom needed a Green Witch in every generation, taking over when her predecessor was no longer strong enough to protect the people of Greater Greensward. Another part of her, however, was so jealous that she got a sour taste in her mouth every time she thought about Chartreuse being able to work magic. It would mean that one of her greatest fears was about to be realized: she, Grassina, would be the untalented nobody in a family of special people.

After reciting the spell, Chartreuse waited expectantly as a few errant bubbles drifted across the water. She'd worn her hair loose that morning, so when she leaned close for a better look, a curl fell forward to trail across the water's surface. Chartreuse wasn't aware of it until a large fish, mistaking her hair for a floating insect, snapped at the curl and yanked. "Ow!" she squeaked as she lost her balance. She fell in the water far enough to drench her face and hair, and might have tumbled in all the way if her mother hadn't grabbed the back of her tunic. When she sat up spluttering, Chartreuse had bits of water weed plastered to her face.

Grassina laughed. "Now, that took talent! I'm sure your suitors will be impressed when they hear what you can do!"

"Don't you dare tell them!" cried Chartreuse, lunging at her sister.

Their mother stepped between the girls. "That's quite enough," Olivene said. "Chartreuse, princesses do not strike their sisters, so stop trying."

"But she's so aggravating, Mother!" complained Chartreuse.

"And as for you, Grassina," Olivene continued. "I expect that you will show discretion and refrain from telling anyone about your sister's lessons."

Grassina started backing away. "I won't say a word as long as no one asks me how Chartreuse's magic is going. But you know that princesses must always tell the truth." Hiking up her skirts, Grassina turned and ran.

"You'd better watch out!" shouted Chartreuse. "When I'm the Green Witch, I'll teach you not to be such a brat!"

"You'll have to get your magic first!" puffed Grassina as she disappeared around the side of the castle. "And I'm not holding my breath until you do!"

Two

King Aldrid and his men were tilting, taking turns riding at the quintain—the figure of a knight that spun around each time they hit it with a lance. Grassina knew that the quintain had been rebuilt that spring, but it already looked battered and ancient. Since the king was an avid jouster, he and his knights practiced nearly every day.

Grassina was passing by when her father rode to the front of the line. Staying well out of the way, she found a good vantage point and stopped to watch. King Aldrid's horse snorted, jerked its head, and danced a few feet to the side. Grassina held her breath as her father shifted his weight in the saddle and leaned forward. Then, moving as if they were one, horse and rider thundered across the hoof-chewed dirt, sending clods flying and stirring up enough dust to create a cloud behind them. The king's lance slammed into the quintain, spinning it as he galloped past while avoiding the flying weight attached to the other side. Bouncing on her toes, Grassina clapped until

11

the palms of her hands stung, although her father was too far away to hear her over the thud of his horse's hooves and the shouted congratulations of his knights.

While the knights debated who would go next, Grassina slipped past the quintain, heading for her tree house. In a copse of trees out of sight of the practice field, it had been her favorite place to play when she was young. Her mother had made it for her to share with Chartreuse, and it was special in ways only an accomplished witch could manage. Although the miniature cottage was nestled in the branches of an oak well above the ground, it was roomier inside than its outside dimensions suggested and had a working fireplace that kept the cottage warm and cozy. Made with magic, the tree house still looked as new as the day it had been built with its sharply pitched roof and arched windows.

Even before Grassina set foot on the ladder, she could smell the wildflower and honey scent that always lingered around the tree house. Her copper finches began to chirp as she started up the rungs, growing louder as she climbed and bursting into song when she reached the platform. Grassina had purchased the birds on a trip to the magic marketplace with her mother. She had wanted to keep them in her chamber, but they had kept her awake the first night with their chattering. The next morning she had moved them to the tree house.

"Good morning, pretty ones," she said. When the

birds chirped back, she copied their song, smiling when they fluttered their wings and chirped louder. Because part of her mother's magic ensured that nothing could enter or leave the tree house without the girls letting it, the birds were uncaged and allowed to fly free.

There were other birds in the room as well. Shortly after Grassina had purchased her two copper birds, Chartreuse had insisted on going to the marketplace. Visiting a different vendor, she'd bought a dozen birds of pale blue glass. She'd also bought a glass branch that she set on the tree-house floor, providing a perch for her precious birds. That had been years ago, and now only five birds remained intact, the rest broken when they flew into the walls or each other.

While the birds fluttered above her, Grassina knelt beside the wooden chest at the foot of one of the tree house's two benches. "You may come out," she said, lifting the lid, "but only for a few minutes. I won't be staying long today."

A small wooden horse whinnied and tossed its head when Grassina reached for it. A rag doll yawned and sat up, wiping its black-dot eyes. Both toys had come from the magic marketplace, gifts from her mother years before. There had also been a tiny chicken made of straw, but it had gotten too close to the fireplace one winter's day and burned itself to ashes. Since that day Grassina had kept the toys shut in the chest when she wasn't there, hoping to keep them out of trouble.

When Grassina had set both toys on the floor, the doll struggled to climb up her leg while the horse trotted around the room, cantering when it reached the long, open space between the two benches, slowing to a walk as it rounded the leg of the table. It was trotting again when its hoof became wedged between two of the floorboards. The horse grew frantic when it stumbled and couldn't get loose. Thrashing and screaming, it might have damaged itself if Grassina hadn't intervened. At first the horse was too frightened for her to touch it, but she calmed it with her voice and gentle hands until it stood still, trembling, and she could pull the hoof free.

"Poor Hector," said the doll, running to throw her arms around the horse's neck. "Are you all right?" she asked.

"He's fine, Marniekins," said Grassina. "Just a little chipped paint."

Hector whuffled his lips, then left to investigate the floor under the bench. Grassina was watching him when she heard someone on the ladder. The copper finches twittered as a head appeared over the top rung. It was Chartreuse, visiting the tree house for the first time in years.

"Princess Chartreuse, is that really you?" squeaked Marniekins. The little doll ran to the princess as fast as her wobbly cloth legs could carry her, falling in a heap when they bent the wrong way. Hector nickered hello and galloped to where Chartreuse stood by the door. On her feet again, Marniekins clambered across the floor to grab hold

14

of the edge of Chartreuse's gown. "Pick me up!" said the doll.

Shoving the doll aside with her foot, Chartreuse crossed to the window and peered out, waving at someone below. "I'm surprised to find you here, Grassina. Torrance and I were going for a walk and heard your voice. Aren't you too old to play with dolls? I'm sure your time would be much better spent learning how to manage a castle or play a musical instrument."

Marniekins had tumbled head over heels, landing in a dusty heap under the bench. She sobbed, curling up in a ball, and wrapped her arms around herself. Unable to make tears, her faded cheeks remained dry. Hector tossed his head and snorted at Chartreuse before trotting after Marniekins. He poked the doll with a consoling nose until she rubbed her eyes.

Grassina glared at Chartreuse. "Now see what you've done!" Peering under the bench, Grassina reached for Marniekins. She cradled the doll in her lap, soothing her as best she could. Marniekins whimpered, hiding her face behind Grassina's hand.

Upset by the turmoil, the copper finches twittered in agitation while Chartreuse's birds fluttered madly overhead. When one of the glass birds collided with a copper finch, a glass wing broke off and the bird fell, shattering on the floor. At the sound, Marniekins howled and buried her face in the cloth of Grassina's gown.

Chartreuse gave the doll a disgusted look. "Don't you dare make me out to be a villain," she said, turning back to Grassina. "They're just dolls. I climbed that ladder to ask you to stay away from my magic lessons. You ruined my lesson today. I was getting close to making the spell work. The magic was building up inside me; I could feel it! If it hadn't been for you, today would have been the day we've all been waiting for."

Grassina glanced up from Marniekins and snorted at the anger on her sister's face. "I've never heard Mother say anything about feeling the magic inside of her. If you felt something, it was probably your breakfast disagreeing with you. And if you're so sure that your magic is about to show itself, I'm sure one day won't make any difference. You'll be able to do the spell tomorrow."

"Not if you're there to distract me! My magic lessons are very important and . . ."

Grassina laughed. "Magic lessons! They aren't lessons unless you can do magic, too. Otherwise they're just demonstrations."

Chartreuse's eyes darkened and her nostrils flared. "It's all a game to you, isn't it? Well, it isn't to me. I take those lessons seriously. Greater Greensward needs a Green Witch; I *have* to learn how to work those spells! You don't need to know about magic, so go play somewhere else, little girl, and leave the important work to the adults!" Turning on her heel, Chartreuse flounced out of

16

the tree house and stomped down the ladder so hard t¹ Grassina could feel the floor of the little house shake.

Long after Chartreuse was gone, Grassina sat on the floor, calming the doll and the horse. Some of what her sister had said stung, perhaps because she was close to being right. Grassina had heard all her life that as long as anyone could remember, there had been only one witch in the family for each generation and that witch had always been the firstborn girl. Since she and everyone else in the family were convinced that she wouldn't have the magic, it seemed only natural for her to make a joke out of it.

Grassina was still stroking Marniekin's flax hair when she realized that the doll was asleep. Hector, too, stood with his eyes closed. Moving carefully so she wouldn't wake them, Grassina carried the toys to the wooden chest and laid them inside. "Sleep tight," she whispered, closing the lid.

Half the afternoon was gone, and she had yet to visit the swamp.

Chartreuse was only two years older than Grassina, and they had once been the best of friends. But after Chartreuse decided that she had to prepare herself to be the Green Witch, she no longer had the time to waste on a younger sister. Grassina began to spend increasing amounts of time on her own, exploring the castle and the area around it. Although she had always known about the swamp, which lay just beyond the practice fields and the woods where the tree house stood, it wasn't until she was on her own that Grassina actually visited it. On the very first visit, Grassina fell in love. After that, no one could keep her away.

Despite her parents' fear that she would become lost or injured, Grassina always managed to slip away when no one was watching. Her parents fought to keep her out of the swamp until the day her father had one of his men follow her to see what she did there. When he reported that she seemed to have an instinct about where to place her feet and that she was more careful than most adults, her father gave her permission to visit the swamp provided she had an escort. Her appointed escorts tried to stay by her side, yet she invariably lost them in the swamp and returned home on her own. More than one adult had to be rescued, although Grassina never did. It wasn't long before no one would go with her. Grassina was ten years old when her parents gave up.

The shy wildlife that Grassina loved to watch, the mysterious pools that could conceal just about anything in their muddy depths, and the graceful willows that hid her in their sheltering boughs called to her in a way that no one else in her family could understand. What Grassina considered mysterious, Chartreuse found frightening. What Grassina found fascinating made her sister turn up her nose in disgust. Unlike her sister, who reveled in the company of others, Grassina appreciated having somewhere she could go alone, away from the eyes, ears, and wagging tongues of the crowded castle, somewhere she could be free to do whatever she pleased. When she wanted to be alone with her thoughts, there was no better place to go than the swamp.

Grassina's first stop was a pond with cattails at one end and a pebbled bank at the other. She watched a turtle sunning itself on a log and an otter chasing fish in the shallower water. When the otter disappeared upstream, Grassina started down a path that wound across the marshy ground and was so faint that only the most experienced tracker could have found it. The path led to the northern side, where the swamp bordered the enchanted forest. She had seen creatures of all kinds drinking from a tree-shaded lake there. Although it wasn't the safest place in the swamp, it was the only spot where the more unusual plant life grew.

As she grew older, Grassina had developed an interest in the flora of the swamp. She had studied with an old woman from a nearby village, an herbalist who was delighted to have a princess as a pupil since it meant that she ate well on lesson days and was paid in real coin. During her years of study with the old woman, Grassina's interest in plants had become a passion, but the old woman had died the year before, leaving Grassina to study on her own. In her mind, that meant spending even more time in the swamp looking for specimens.

Although Grassina loved the swamp, she wasn't blind

to its dangers and was particularly careful when visiting the lake that bordered the enchanted forest. Once, while picking leaves from a variety of marsh mallow that grew at the edge of the lake, she had heard a shrill cry coming from the tall reeds between her and the forest. Looking up, she had seen a flock of crows descending on the reeds and whatever creature they hid. Armed only with a few stones she'd found on the ground, Grassina had gone to investigate. A doe, mauled by something in the forest, had wandered into the swamp to die. Although she was hidden from most eyes, the crows had found her and were impatient to begin feeding. The doe was close to death when Grassina saw her, but alive enough to turn her head. Their eyes met; one look was enough. As the doe lay her head on the ground again, Grassina threw her first stone into the flock of crows, being careful not to hit the deer. The birds squawked and flew off as one stone after another hurtled into their midst, missing most, but hitting enough to frighten them. Grassina had stayed to chase away birds even after the doe was no longer moving. She would have stayed all day if a bear attracted by the scent of blood hadn't shuffled out of the forest.

Knowing that her poorly aimed stones would do little more than irritate a bear, Grassina retreated farther into the swamp. The very next day she collected stones again. Instead of skipping them across a pond, she threw them at the gnarled knot in a tree trunk, hitting the tree but only rarely the knot. The next day she was back again, staying until her arm was sore and her aim was better. Within a month she could hit whatever target she chose. Within two months she could do it while running. Although she rarely needed to use the stones, it made her feel better to know that she could.

Fortunately, on this particular day she saw no sign of anything larger than a deer in the vicinity, so she continued on, searching for certain plants. Finding a specimen with blue-flowered spikes that had opened its blooms since her last visit, she picked one stem, leaving the rest to grow and spread. She was tucking her new find into the leather sack she'd brought when she caught the faintest whiff of smoke.

"There must be a dragon nearby," Grassina murmured. It was time to head for home.

Tilting practice was ending when she passed the field, so she sought out her father and joined him as he passed his horse's reins to his squire.

"Hello, sweetling," he said when Grassina appeared at his side. "I thought I saw you coming. What have you been up to today?"

As they started toward the castle, Grassina told him about her morning, including her conversation with Chartreuse. "It isn't fair," she said, kicking a pebble with the toe of her shoe. "Chartreuse is going to be the queen and the Green Witch just because she's older than me. All I'm going to do is marry some old, boring suitor that Chartreuse doesn't want."

King Aldrid tugged on his daughter's braid. "Chartreuse may think that fortune favors her now, but give her a few years and she'll think that you're the lucky one. With either of those titles comes a great deal of responsibility. Bearing both titles can be overwhelming. Just ask your mother. She never wanted to be the Green Witch. Given a choice, she would have preferred to do only small magic the way many of the village witches do."

"Really? If I were a witch, I'd specialize in big spells that would make a big difference and really help people. I wouldn't waste my time with the little ones like spelling my name with bubbles. But I don't understand why Mother never told us how she felt about magic."

Her father shrugged. "She knew that your sister would be the next Green Witch someday, so she wanted to let Chartreuse form her own opinion about magic. Seeing how the responsibility of being the Green Witch had affected her mother was what turned your mother against the job."

"What did it do to Grandmother?"

"We all thought your grandmother was crazy; your mother thought it was because of the things she had to do to protect the kingdom as the Green Witch. The monsters she had to face . . . The horrible things they did if she wasn't there in time . . . It was enough to give anyone nightmares."

"But the Green Witch is the most powerful witch in the kingdom. She can handle anything!" said Grassina.

"Yes, but at a tremendous cost. The horrors she has to deal with . . . Not to mention that her responsibilities as the Green Witch take precedence over her private life. Your mother never got to spend time with you the way she would have liked. Even now, she has no time for all the little things that she used to enjoy so much."

"I didn't realize . . ."

"As for whom you'll marry . . . You'll have a say in choosing your future husband. I'll see to that. Chartreuse, however, will marry whomever your mother and I decide would make the most suitable husband for someone in her position. The man who marries the queen of Greater Greensward must meet the kingdom's needs before his wife's. Whoever marries the Green Witch must not be someone who would try to misuse her magic. Chartreuse's choices are far more limited than yours will be."

"You're not saying that just to make me feel better?" asked Grassina, studying her father's face.

Her father laughed and shook his head. "I wouldn't dare try to convince you of anything. I know you too well. Just don't let Chartreuse upset you when she talks about her brilliant future. Nothing is ever exactly what we expect it to be."

Three

ou've changed and I don't like it," said the queen on the other side of the closed door. Her voice was ill-tempered and angry, which was unusual for her. Grassina had been about to knock, but she dropped her hand and hesitated, torn between wanting to hear what her mother said next and knowing how upset the queen would be if she knew that someone was eavesdropping.

"I don't know what you mean," said King Aldrid, sounding puzzled.

"You were so attentive when we first met. Don't you remember singing love songs outside my window at night until my father threatened to have you dragged off to the dungeon? You gave me so many gifts that I didn't know what to do with them all. You even begged me for a lock of my hair to keep by your heart. After we were married, you took me to tournaments and on that grand tour. We were so happy together, and you promised that it would never end."

"I remember," he said. "We were young then and didn't have the responsibilities that we have now."

"Don't talk to me about responsibilities! I know exactly what's expected of me by you and everyone else in this kingdom. All I'm asking for is a little romance ... some sign that you still love and cherish me and that I'm still important to you and not just because of what I do for our kingdom. I want you to be the man you used to be. I want to feel the way I used to feel."

"I didn't know you weren't happy," said King Aldrid. "You've never said anything before. What brought this on?"

"Nothing, really. I was talking to Chartreuse and I remembered how it once was, that's all. She's so bright-eyed and certain of her future, like I was at her age. I suppose I just need to know ... Are you still the Aldrid I married? Do you still love me the way you once did?"

"Of course I do!" the king said, beginning to sound irritated.

"You certainly never show it!" The queen's voice was louder, as if she were coming closer. Grassina stepped back a pace, not wanting to be caught listening.

"You have to tell me what you want. I can't read your mind!" said the king.

"That much is obvious!" The queen had almost reached the door. "You never even *tell* me that you love me anymore."

"I shouldn't have to say it."

"Perhaps not, but it would be nice if you did it without having to."

Grassina's heart was pounding when she darted down the corridor and slipped behind a wall hanging that covered a small, drafty alcove. Peeking out from behind the hanging, she searched her mother's face as the queen passed by and was dismayed to see tears streaking her cheeks. As a child, hearing her parents argue had frightened Grassina, perhaps because they did it so rarely. It upset her even now, although she couldn't have explained why. Talking to someone about it might help, but it had to be someone who felt the same way she did. Only one name came to mind.

Grassina often forgot just how big the castle was until she had to find someone. She looked for Chartreuse in her chamber, but it was empty. Even her sister's new kitten was gone. Chartreuse wasn't in the Great Hall either, nor their mother's chamber, nor any other room where she might usually be found. To her surprise, she finally found her in the kitchen.

A few years before, Grassina had developed a love for cooking and had persuaded the cooks to give her lessons. She still visited the kitchen often to try her hand at new dishes, but as far as she knew, her older sister had never set foot in the kitchen. Grassina could tell from the sour expressions on the cooks' faces that they weren't pleased about Chartreuse's current visit.

Chartreuse was standing at the long table where she'd shoved aside a mound of vegetables, leaving a cleared space for her to work. A book, a bowl of flour, a saltcellar, a lump of butter, and a dozen apples lay on the table in front of her. An orange-striped kitten sat on the table at Chartreuse's elbow, lapping a bowl of milk. Supper was hours away, but roasts were already turning on the spit, making Grassina's mouth water from the aroma of the sizzling juices. She was wondering if the cook might give her something to tide her over when Chartreuse began to read aloud from the book.

> Pour the flour and the salt.
> Drop in a bit of lard.
> Mix it till it's nice and smooth.
> Add water—it's not hard.

Although Grassina was watching carefully, nothing seemed to be happening. "A cooking spell," she murmured. "I wonder where she found that."

> Roll it flat and roll it wide.
> Cut squares with a blade.
> Lay the apple slices there.
> Don't stop—it's nearly made.

The ingredients hadn't budged from the table. "It's not working," said Grassina. "Why are you going on with the spell if it's not doing what it's supposed to? And why are you wasting your time on a cooking spell in the first place? You can cook without magic. Now if *I* were trying to do magic, I'd do something big that could make a real difference that I couldn't make any other way."

Chartreuse looked up from the table to glare at her sister. "If I wanted your opinion, I'd ask for it. Go away. I'm busy."

"But I need to talk to you," Grassina said, glancing at the cooks and their score of assistants. Although none were looking in the sisters' direction, they were all working so quietly that she was sure they were listening. "It's about our parents," she told Chartreuse in a fierce whisper.

"Didn't this afternoon's conversation sink in at all?" asked Chartreuse. "I don't want you anywhere near me when I'm doing my magic!" Picking up the book, she pointedly turned her back on her sister.

Chartreuse's kitten licked its paw, then used it to wipe its face. Cat hairs floated in a sunbeam coming through one of the windows set high in the wall. Grassina crinkled her nose when some of the hairs drifted into the bowl of flour. She picked up the kitten to set it on the floor, and it mewed, earning her a nasty look from Chartreuse.

"I have to talk to you," said Grassina. "This is important. They've been fighting."

Chartreuse slammed the book on the table and spun around. "So you think that what I'm doing isn't important? Get out of here and leave me alone! And that goes for my kitten, too. I never said you could touch it." Giving her sister a nasty look, she snatched the kitten off the floor and set it on the table. The kitten backed away, bumping into the bowl of flour. The bowl overturned and the flour splashed out, coating the kitten from head to toe. Howling, the kitten jumped to the floor and dashed around the kitchen, leaving a white, powdery trail.

A scullery maid was carrying a bucket of water when the kitten ran under her feet, tripping her. The bucket went flying, the water gushing over the spitted roasts, drenching them and extinguishing the fire. The head cook roared and, grabbing a broom, flailed at the kitten. Terrified, the kitten tore out of the kitchen and down the corridor toward the Great Hall. Chartreuse snatched up her book and ran after her pet. Grassina grabbed some apples and was only a few paces behind.

Although most of King Aldrid's hounds had gone outside to pester the stable boys, one hound had stayed behind to take a nap by the fireplace. Woken by the still-yowling kitten, the hound scrambled to its feet and took off after the dusty white ball of fluff. Bigger and faster than the kitten, the hound would have caught it if, just as its jaws were about to close, the flour puffing off the warm, furry body hadn't tickled the hound's nose. The hound sneezed, giving the kitten enough time to launch itself onto one of Queen Olivene's prized tapestries decorating the closest wall. Its needlelike claws dug into the woven fabric as the kitten climbed until it was too high for the hound or anyone else to reach. This didn't discourage the hound, who leaped at the tapestry, barking hysterically. Dragged down by the weight of the hound, the tapestry tore at the top where it was fastened to the wall and began to sag.

Chartreuse glanced at Grassina. "Now see what you've done!"

"You're blaming me?" said Grassina. "It's your kitten!"

"We were fine until you came in!"

The hound jumped again, scrabbling at the tapestry with its paws.

"I'll get the hound," said Grassina. "You get your kitten."

Grassina reached for the hound's collar, but the animal snapped at her when she came close. She looked to see if her sister was having any better luck. Chartreuse was thumbing through her book, licking her finger before she turned each page.

Grassina was still trying to decide how to approach the hound when Chartreuse began to read a spell for getting things down from high places using a loud, decisive voice. Grassina shook her head. "I can't believe she's trying magic now!" she muttered.

While Chartreuse concentrated on the spell, Grassina looked around for something she could use to scare off the hound. She was about to go back to the kitchen when she remembered the apples. "This should do it," she said, hefting one in her hand.

The apple hit the hound in the ribs, surprising it so that it took off yelping with its tail between its legs. When the kitten still didn't come down, Grassina threw another so that it hit the tapestry directly above the kitten's head. Startled, the kitten pulled its claws free and fell. Chartreuse took her eyes from her book just as the kitten landed in Grassina's arms.

"Did you see that?" Chartreuse asked, her voice a high squeak. "Did you see what I just did? My magic finally worked! I told you today was my day!"

Grassina tried to keep a straight face, but the twitching of her lips almost betrayed her. "Yes, indeed. The way that cat came down was pure magic. Congratulations, Chartreuse. I didn't know you had it in you!"

"But I did!" said Chartreuse. Clapping her hands, she twirled on her toes and did a little jig. "I did it! I did it! I have to go tell Mother right away."

The pages sitting at a nearby table were trying hard not to laugh, but when one snorted with the effort, they all broke up, guffawing and slapping the table. Princes Torrance and Pietro had just come into the room when Chartreuse noticed them. She waved and smiled again before turning back to the pages. Her smile evaporated as she said, "Why are you laughing? Did I say something funny?" Her eyes narrowed when they grinned back at her. "I didn't do it, did I? It was something you did, wasn't it?" She turned to glare at Grassina accusingly.

Grassina nodded, then giggled in spite of herself. "Maybe today wasn't really your day after all."

"You are so immature," Chartreuse said, looking from Grassina to the still-laughing pages.

"At least I know my limitations," Grassina murmured as her sister stalked off.

Four

The next morning, Queen Olivene sent for her daughters, telling them to meet her by the moat. Chartreuse arrived first and looked disappointed when her sister appeared on the drawbridge. "What are you doing here?" she asked.

"The same thing you are," said Grassina. "Don't bother telling me to go away. Mother told me to come."

Chartreuse was about to reply when Queen Olivene stepped off the end of the drawbridge. "Come along, girls. We have much to do today. I've invited you to join us, Grassina, because Sophronia has gone home. She told me there's no use trying to teach someone deportment and the courtly graces if that person can't be found. Finished with your lesson, indeed!"

"Well, I was," said Grassina. "Lady Sophronia just didn't know it."

"And so I'm stuck with you," muttered Chartreuse.

"It could be worse," said Grassina. "It could be Prince Rinaldo."

"I hope we can get through this fast," Chartreuse said as the girls turned to follow their mother. "The princes are waiting for our morning walk."

"All of them?" asked Grassina.

"Of course," said Chartreuse. "You wouldn't want me to play favorites, would you?"

"Not yet," Grassina said under her breath. "You're having too much fun the way it is."

The queen took the girls down the road leading away from the castle. When they reached a farmer's hayfield, they picked their way through the stubble left over from a recent cutting until they reached the overgrown thicket that divided the field from the one beyond it. Using an impromptu spell, Olivene cleared away a strip of ground facing the thicket and had the girls sit on either side of her.

"Now listen carefully, Chartreuse," said the queen. "I'm going to teach you a spell to call animals. This spell is longer than the one I showed you yesterday. Pay particular attention to the tone of voice I use. That's critical in a number of spells."

Resting her hands in her lap, the queen opened her mouth to begin, but a voice called out, "Pardon me, my dear. I must speak with you." The king was walking toward them with one hand behind his back, looking pensive the

34

way he did when considering a serious problem. "Girls, please leave us. Your mother and I need to be alone."

Gathering their skirts around them, the girls took their leave, although they didn't go far. When Chartreuse would have returned to the castle, Grassina stopped her, saying, "We can't go home. They're going to fight, I know it."

"It's none of our business," hissed Chartreuse.

"Of course it is," said Grassina. "They're our parents. Everything they do is our business. Did you see the expression on Father's face? He looked odd."

"Fine, we'll listen in, but only because we care."

"Precisely," said Grassina.

Moving as quietly as they could, the girls crept through an opening in the thicket and down its length until they could see their parents while remaining hidden.

". . . a lesson," said the queen. "Chartreuse is doing so well at memorizing the spells."

"Very nice," King Aldrid said, sounding as if he wasn't really paying attention. He cleared his throat with a loud *harumph* before saying, "I thought about what you said yesterday. I wrote a poem for you. I know it isn't very good, but I never was much at writing, although you always seemed to like whatever I wrote. Here it is."

> *Though I forget from day to day*
> *To find the words I ought to say,*

You're half my heart and half my soul.
Without your love I can't be whole.
So please forgive me if I fail
To say how much I love you.

"That was so sappy!" whispered Grassina. "I can't believe he said that!"

Chartreuse sighed. "I think it was terribly romantic."

Tears glittered in the queen's eyes. "It was perfect," she said, smiling up at him.

"I got you these myself," he said, pulling a bouquet of wildflowers from behind his back. "I didn't have time to get you anything else. I hope you like them."

The queen gasped, her eyes growing wide when he laid the bouquet in her lap. The petal of a daisy brushed the back of her hand, and a breeze sprang up, carrying the heavy scent of roses and lilies, although there were none in the bouquet.

Grassina suddenly felt uneasy. She turned to look around her, thinking that the weather might be changing or someone might be coming, but nothing had happened as far as she could tell. The sun was still shining in a cloudless sky, the birds were still twittering in the thicket, the fields were still empty, and her parents . . .

It was then that she noticed that her mother had begun to change. Her softly curling strawberry blond hair was becoming lank and dull, turning the color of wet mud. Her well-shaped nose was growing long and hooked, nearly meeting her increasingly pointy chin. The once-flawless skin of her cheeks was becoming bumpy and coarse, and her gentle eyes were now beady and piercing.

Unfortunately, her appearance wasn't the only thing that had changed. "What are you staring at?" she rasped. The voice that had been declared the sweetest in the kingdom now sounded like a rusty saw sharpening on a dull whetstone.

Grassina and Chartreuse gasped behind the concealing thicket and reached for each other's hands. King Aldrid's sun-bronzed cheeks went pale. "Then it was true," he said, his voice hoarse. "Your mother told me of the curse, but you said she was crazy. I thought she was, too. She was afraid of so many things—men wearing pointy hats, shadows in the snow, red shoes on little girls. We never thought any of it was real."

"What are you yammering on about, you addle-pated fool?" demanded Queen Olivene. "And men say women talk too much."

"If only I'd realized that the old woman was right about the curse. She said that if you touched a flower after your sixteenth birthday you'd turn into a horrible hag. To think that it's my fault that you've—"

"Enough of this blathering!" the queen snapped. Pointing her finger at her husband, she chanted,

Go hide inside your hidey hole,
You mumbling, bumbling rat.
Stay in the dungeon till I say
You've had enough of that.

There was a squeak like a rat might make, and King
Aldrid disappeared.

Chartreuse cried out and hid her face in her hands, while
Grassina jumped to her feet, shouting, "No!"

Queen Olivene's head whipped around. "So you were
spying on me? I hope you got a good eyeful."

Ignoring the thorns that tore at her clothes, Grassina
forced her way through the thicket. "Where's Father?" she
asked. "What have you done with him?"

"I sent him to the dungeon, where he can talk all he
wants and I won't have to listen to him." Olivene chuckled, making her long nose quiver. "Serves him right. He
didn't say anything that I wanted to hear."

"What happened to you?" asked Grassina, unwanted
tears thickening her voice. "Are you going to be like this
for good?"

"For good or ill, who's to say? Why, do you have a
problem with it?"

Grassina held out her hand to the queen. "I want you
back the way you were!"

Queen Olivene hopped to her feet and stuck out a long, crooked finger. Prodding Grassina's collarbone, she said, "Well, we" *poke*, "don't always" *poke*, "get what we want." With one last poke, she pushed so hard that Grassina fell backward into the thicket, crying out as the thorns scratched her.

Hot tears stung the cuts on Grassina's cheeks. She sobbed, turning her head aside so she wouldn't have to look at Olivene's awful, leering face.

Olivene's lips curved down in disgust. "Look at that! Frightened of your own shadow! Why, you're as scared as a rabbit!" An idea occurred to her, changing her expression to one of glee. "In that case," she said, "if you're going to act like one, maybe you should be one and see what it's really like." Pointing her finger at Grassina, Olivene chanted,

> Turn this silly, wretched girl
> Into a frightened rabbit.
> Let her see how she would feel
> Were fear a lifelong habit.

"No!" cried Grassina, struggling to get out of the way of the crooked finger, but the thorns held her in place like a skewered roast in the kitchen. She cried out when her skin began to prickle and her skull began to itch. When the world seemed to tilt, she shut her eyes and tried to hold back a sudden swell of nausea.

39

Although Grassina had never known her mother to turn herself into an animal or talk about it if she had, she had seen her turn someone into a dog once. A soldier had beaten a homeless hound, so the queen had changed the man into a small, ugly cur until he'd agreed to mend his ways. The soldier was a changed man after that, but it wasn't what had made the biggest impression on Grassina. It was the way he had looked while he transformed, shrinking in some ways, growing in others, his clothes melting into him as his fur sprouted and his hands and feet became paws. It had frightened her at the time, watching the man change while his expression vacillated from horrified to pained and back again. The experience had given her nightmares for weeks, but she'd never thought she'd have to live through it herself.

Thankfully, the pain wasn't nearly what Grassina had expected. In fact, it didn't hurt exactly, although it did feel extremely odd. As her hands and feet curled into paws and her ears lengthened and moved to the top of her head, she kept waiting for the pain to begin. It hurt a bit when her body shrank, but it was more of an ache than a pain and didn't last very long.

Her ears had nearly stopped growing when she heard a chicken squawking and a nasty, rasping laugh. Frantic, Grassina wiggled free of the last few thorns that held her in place and looked around her. There was no sign of her mother or Chartreuse, but that didn't mean they weren't close by. A snapped twig made her go deeper into the thicket where the leaves concealed her from anyone outside.

Learning how to hop the way rabbits do wasn't easy in the confines of a thicket. Grassina managed, however, tripping only a few times and hitting her head only once. She found it hard to avoid catching her ears on thorns, and her fluffy tail was almost yanked off after it got snagged, making her move even more cautiously.

When she heard a whisper of sound nearby, Grassina had already worked her way so far into the thicket that all she could see was a wall of green. She crouched down to make herself as small as possible and froze, listening to the muted rustling, scraping, and scratching common to a thicket. It occurred to her that she wasn't alone and that some of the other animals might be bigger and meaner than a rabbit. Any predator that came along would be unlikely to know or care that she was really a thirteen-year-old girl.

Unfortunately, Grassina had always had a vivid imagination. With each new sound, she pictured all sorts of creatures that could live in a thicket, any one of which might enjoy a nice rabbit meal. When nothing appeared, she began to worry about other things like whether her mother's transformation was temporary or permanent and whether the queen would come looking for her. She thought about her father and how he must feel, then began to worry about what would become of her family if her mother didn't change back. When nothing new happened, she worried that she was going to have to spend the rest of her life as a rabbit.

"Oh dear," said a voice from somewhere close by. Grassina pricked up her ears, swiveling them in the direction of the sound. She froze again when she heard the whisper of something brushing against the leaves. "And I thought thingss couldn't get any worsse," moaned the voice. "What should I do now?"

Although it wasn't Chartreuse's voice, it had to be her. Who else could be in this thicket, talking in a way Grassina could understand? Their mother must have changed both of her daughters at the same time. And if it was Chartreuse, it sounded as if she'd been hurt, perhaps by the magic that had changed her.

Moving as quietly as she could, Grassina crept through the hedge, listening for her sister. There was a sound—over there. It was close, too. If it was Chartreuse, whatever she had been turned into should be visible by now. Grassina couldn't see her, but she did smell an unfamiliar, musky scent. She was watching the play of dappled light on the shadowy green foliage when a long narrow head moved, two glistening black eyes looked her way, and the shape that had blended into the thicket so well suddenly became apparent.

"Chartreuse?" Grassina whispered to the snake. "Is that you?"

"Go away!" whispered the snake. "Don't come near me. Ssomething bad will happen if you do!"

Grassina hopped closer. "Don't be silly, Chartreuse. It's me, Grassina. What's wrong with your tail?"

The snake had twisted around itself until the last few inches of its tail rested on the top coil. Part of it looked flatter than the rest, and whole rows of bright green scales were missing. "You don't want to know. It'ss a very long sstory."

"I don't have anywhere to go," Grassina said, stretching out on the cool soil to listen.

The little snake sighed. "If you inssisst, but I warned you! It'ss my bad luck, you ssee. I've been plagued with it ssince before I wass hatched. My mother abandoned me, sso I wass all alone in the world when I broke out of my shell. I wass crawling to another branch when I fell out of my tree. It took me an entire morning to climb back up. The next day a witch named Mudine ssnatched me from my jungle where I was nice and warm, dropped me in a bassket, and whisked me away to her cottage in thesse cold, cold woodss. She locked me in a cage and fed me inssectss that made my sstomach hurt.

"Then bad thingss began happening to her. A sstorm made her roof leak and ruined her magic bookss. A rat wandered in and ate her mosst important herbss. Her potion sscorched when she took a nap. That'ss when she told me it wass all my fault; she ssaid that her bad luck began the day

43

she brought me home. She called me a jinx, and I knew she was right. Bad luck followss me wherever I go."

"I'm sorry to hear that," said Grassina as she took a step backward. Apparently, this wasn't Chartreuse after all.

"Yessterday a hairy monsster broke into the cottage and ssmashed everything. The witch wass out, you ssee, or she would have turned him into a mousse and fed him to me. When the monsster broke my cage, I thought I'd finally be free. I wass almosst out the door when he sstepped on my tail. I thought he wass going to kill me, but he changed hiss mind and I got away after all. I sstill have bad luck, though. I can't go far with a tail like thiss. Ah, I ssee you undersstand. That'ss it, move away from me. Maybe my bad luck won't hurt you if you leave now."

Grassina kept backing away until she bumped into the thicket behind her. Despite what the creature said, it wasn't its bad luck that she found frightening. "You're a real snake!" she said, her eyes widening as she realized something else. "Then why can I understand everything you're saying?"

"Why wouldn't you be able to undersstand me, unlesss . . . Is there ssomething wrong with the way I talk?" the snake asked, becoming agitated. "Are my wordss getting sslurred? Iss my voice getting faint? I'm going to die now, aren't I? The end iss near. I can feel it! It'ss my bad luck, I tell you. That monsster musst have hurt me more than I thought when it sstepped on my tail!"

"I doubt it. You sound fine. It's just that I'm really a human girl, not a rabbit, and I shouldn't be able to understand you . . . unless . . . Is it because I *am* a rabbit now?"

"You're crazy," said the snake. "That explainss a lot. Only a crazy rabbit would want to hear my sstory. Monkeyss are crazy, and if you're like them . . ."

"I'm not crazy. I'm a human girl who . . ."

"You're no human; you're a rabbit. Jusst look at that little twitchy nosse and fluffy puff of a tail! I think that . . . Shh! What wass that?"

A leaf rustled. Fur brushed a twig. A padded paw scraped an exposed root. Grassina raised her head to sniff the air. There was a new scent, like her own rabbity smell, yet completely different. This scent set her whiskers quivering and made the fur along her spine bristle. Whatever the creature was, she already didn't like it.

Turning her head ever so slowly, Grassina glimpsed a flash of russet fur and the tip of a pointed ear. It was a fox, and it was only a few feet away inside the tangled thicket.

"Thiss iss the end," whispered the snake. "Now ssomeone iss going to die becausse of my bad luck. I can't sslither fasst with my tail like thiss, and you're crazier than a butterfly that thinkss it can sswim. We don't sstand a chance!"

Caught between the instinct to run and her desire to help a creature in need, Grassina paused for only a second before saying, "I'm not crazy, and I'm not leaving you here to die. There must be something we can do." Her eyes fell on a broken twig. When she tried to pick it up, she had to use both paws to hold it, being careful not to prick herself on the wicked-looking thorns.

The twig wobbled as Grassina raised it between her paws and turned to face the fox. Smiling, the fox skirted a prickly branch while its eyes flicked from her to the snake. "What have we here?" it said, licking its lips.

"You don't want to fool with me," Grassina said.

The fox smirked. "And why is that?"

"Because I have this!" she said. Raising the twig over her head, she hopped once and brought it down on the fox's skull as hard as she could. The fox jerked its head away, but Grassina followed, raining blows on it with the thorny twig.

"What are you doing?" the fox barked. "You're a rabbit. You're supposed to be afraid! Stop that! Ow! Ow!"

The fox dodged, trying to evade her blows. Grassina was still walloping the animal when her skin began to tingle, her paws to prickle, and her ears to ache. She paused and took a deep breath, but her vision blurred, making it hard to see when the fox turned to face her, its lips curled back in a snarl. Shaking her head to clear it made her feel woozy, so she almost didn't notice the fox tensing its muscles to pounce. When she did, she swung at the fox one last time even though she was feeling so light-headed that she was afraid she might faint. She was halfway through her swing when her paws lost their grip on the twig; the tingling had grown until she could feel nothing else.

Grassina's entire body shimmered, but she had her eyes closed, so she didn't see it. Nor did she see the horrified look on the fox's face when she began to change.

The fox turned tail and ran when Grassina's body began to push the thorns aside, breaking some and bending others as she grew. The thorns scratched and bit into her flesh as she returned to her normal size and shape, leaving trickles of blood on her face, hands, and clothes. When the tingling stopped, she felt the thorn-inflicted pain in a rush of sensation that made her cry out. Her eyes fluttered open and she flinched; the thorns were so thick around her that she was afraid to move. Biting her lip at the pain of each new prick and scrape, she pushed the twigs aside as she forced her way through the thicket.

"Well, I'll be . . . ," whispered the little green snake at her feet.

Grassina looked down. "I can still understand you!" she said. "Now do you believe me? I told you I was a human." Something rustled in the thicket only a few yards away. After glancing in that direction, Grassina turned back to the snake. "I don't want to leave you here to get eaten. Come with me and I'll . . ."

The snake drew back, rearranging its coils deeper under the protective thorns. "Pleasse don't try to hurt me! Issn't it bad enough that my tail iss ssquashed?"

Grassina was aghast. "I don't want to hurt you! I have to go home now and see my family, but I don't want to leave you here. If you go with me, I can keep you safe while your tail heals. You won't bite me or anything if I pick you up?"

"Well, you did protect me from that fox," said the snake. "I ssupposse I can trusst you. But I have to warn you that if you take me with you, my bad luck will come, too."

"You don't need to worry about that," said Grassina. "I don't believe in bad luck." Gritting her teeth, she touched the snake, expecting it to feel cold and slimy. Instead it felt nice, not cool, but not exactly warm either. Its scales were smooth, and it tickled when it slid across her palm and wrapped itself around her wrist.

"Ssay," said the snake. "You're not a witch, are you? You're not going to sstick me in a kettle with toe of bat and ear of rat or ssome other dissgussting combination?"

Grassina laughed and shook her head. "You don't need to worry about me. I don't have a lick of magic. I told you, I just want to keep you safe." Pushing aside the last branch, she stepped out of the thicket and stopped to tug her gown free of the thorns. She looked around, afraid of what she might see. The farmer's field was empty except for a flock of scavenging crows; there was no sign of either her sister or her mother. She would have to go home to find out what had happened to her family.

Over the years, she had learned enough about magic to realize that because her mother had cast the spell that changed her, Olivene had to be the one to change her back. She had reverted to her human form, so perhaps her mother's own transformation had been only temporary and she was her normal self again. But if she wasn't . . . Grassina began to hurry, taking long ground-eating strides as she thought about her father's disappearance. And then there was Chartreuse. Who knew what their mother might have done to her?

Grassina would have to tend to the snake first, of course. "Hold on tight. I don't want to drop you."

"I wouldn't blame you if you did. It would jusst be my bad luck again. But I should be fine. I *wass* hatched in a tree, after all. You know, you're the firsst human I've ever talked to. Mudine talked *at* me, but she never tried to talk *to* me."

"And you're the first snake I've ever wanted to talk to," Grassina said, still amazed that she could converse with an animal.

Five

"What are you doing?" demanded Grassina, ducking out of her sister's way.

Chartreuse waved the broom handle, swatting at a web and ripping it down the center. A spider dangled from one of the broken threads. "Vandals! Thieves!" it shouted in a voice no louder than a whisper.

"That should be obvious," said Chartreuse. "Mother told us to collect spiders' webs. Do you know of a better way?"

Grassina put her hand on the broom so that her sister couldn't swing it again. "You don't have to be so rough. We could try asking for them."

"Ask who?" Chartreuse glanced at the stable boy mucking out a nearby stall. "I'm not asking him, if that's what you mean."

Grassina shook her head. "Ask the spiders, of course. The webs belong to them."

"You want to talk to spiders?" Chartreuse sounded incredulous.

"You could do it if you'd like. I think talking to animals is fun."

"You would," said Chartreuse. "But I don't. It's beneath a royal princess to talk to animals. We have a responsibility to our subjects to maintain some decorum. If you'd paid attention to Lady Sophronia, you'd know that we are supposed to set examples for our less fortunate subjects."

"Something awful happened to you when Mother turned you into a chicken, didn't it? You never did tell me what it was like."

Chartreuse gave her such a venomous look that it could have wilted plants. "I told you never to mention it again! It was a nightmare, and I don't want to talk about it!"

Soon after returning home, Grassina had discovered that she hadn't been the only one to have a transformation spell cast on her. Holding up her hands in surrender, she said, "All right, I'm sorry! But if you won't talk to spiders, at least let me try."

"Even you can't think that—"

"We shouldn't use a stick anyway. Did you see how it tore the web? We have to be gentle with them. Mother wants us to keep the webs intact."

Chartreuse sighed. "Then go ahead and do it your

way. I want to get this over with so I can go to bed. I have plans for the morning and need to get up early."

"I just bet you do," muttered Grassina. Spotting another web near the ceiling, she waved her hand at it, calling, "Yoo hoo! Over here."

The spider crouching in the center of the web glared down at them. When it spoke, its voice was scarcely louder than the breathing of the horses in the closest stalls. Grassina wouldn't have heard it if she hadn't been trying her hardest. "Stay away from me, you monsters," said the spider. "I saw what you did to Inez's web."

"I'm sorry," said Grassina. "That was a mistake. It won't happen again."

"You bet it was a mistake," the spider said, waving a leg in the air for emphasis. "That was a beautiful web! Inez is known throughout the stable for her craftsmanship."

"I'm sure she is. I've never seen such lovely webs as the ones I've found here. That's why my mother sent us to get them. She said they were the best in all the land, and she needs them for a very special project."

"I thought we came to the stable because we didn't know where else to look," murmured Chartreuse.

"Shh!" said Grassina, darting an angry glance at her sister. Turning back to the spider, she smiled and said as graciously as she could, "We've come to ask if we might have a selection of your finest webs."

"What sort of special project?" asked the spider, sounding interested in spite of itself.

"Don't you dare listen to her, Corinne," whispered the spider named Inez. "You can't trust a web beater."

"She didn't beat your web," said Corinne. "The other one did."

Inez turned from Grassina to Chartreuse. "They all look alike to me."

"Tell me about the project," Corinne said again.

"Oh, right, the project." Grassina thought fast, trying to come up with something convincing. "My mother is the queen. She's made a wager with another queen that our spiders are finer weavers than any human in her kingdom. Of course Mother wants the best webs she can find to show the other queen—"

"Then it's no wonder you came here," said Corinne. "But you were going about it all wrong. Here, I'll show you." The spider darted to the edge of the web and worked one of the anchoring threads free. "You can have this one. It's one of my best efforts, if I do say so myself."

"Don't do it, Corinne!" shouted Inez. "They don't deserve it."

"Stop being an old stick in the web," said Corinne, loosening a second thread. "I've heard about contests like this. The spiders always win if their webs are half decent. I'm giving the queen the best webs we have." Working on one thread after another, she freed the web until it began to sag.

Olivene had made the girls boil vinegar to wash the webs, then gave them a gray powder to mix with the vinegar, saying, "That should do the trick!" The resulting concoction had smelled so strong that Chartreuse had made Grassina lug the pail to the stable, saying that the odor gave her a headache. Grassina crinkled her nose at the smell as she held up the pail to catch Corinne's falling web.

"Is this going to take much longer?" Chartreuse asked, stifling a yawn. "It's getting late, and I would like to get to bed sometime tonight."

"How many more do you need?" the spider asked Grassina. "Morris! Francine! Your webs should do very well. The queen will need one of Astoria's special weaves, too. Tori, if you undo that end, I'll get started on this one."

By the time the spiders had finished donating their webs for the queens' wager, Grassina had collected more than two dozen. Chartreuse waited impatiently at the stable door while Grassina thanked the spiders.

"That was some story you made up," Chartreuse said as her sister joined her.

"I know, I know, I shouldn't have lied, but what did you expect me to tell them—give us your webs so our mother can use them in a potion? I'm sure that would have gone over well."

Chartreuse patted her sister on the back. "Don't be so prickly. I thought your story was good."

"Maybe," said Grassina, "but I didn't like deceiving them that way."

"Don't let it worry you. They're just bugs."

"So it's all right for a princess to lie to certain people?"

"Certainly not, but spiders aren't people, are they? Now, let's finish these horrid webs. I'm sick of them already."

"Where should we wash them?" asked Grassina.

"Your chamber will do. The smell will keep me awake if we do it in mine. Your room already reeks of all those plants you have drying."

"I'd rather have it smell like herbs than the way that kitten makes your room stink," Grassina muttered as she shifted the weight of the heavy bucket from one hand to the other.

Whatever the powder was that their mother had given them, it kept the webs from clumping or dissolving and made them sparkle as they sloshed around in the pail. Grassina's burden seemed to grow heavier as she climbed the stairs, and she had to stop now and then to rest. Chartreuse finally offered to take a turn, but she did it grudgingly and complained the entire time.

The stars were shining outside Grassina's window when the girls reached her room. Rather than find someone to light her candles for her, Grassina borrowed a flame from a torch in the hall and lit them one by one. A draft from the window made the drying plants hanging from her ceiling rustle and carried their pungent odor down to the girls. Chartreuse wrinkled her nose, but Grassina liked the smell and turned her face up with a sigh.

"What are you waiting for?" said Chartreuse. "I don't have time for this. Don't you realize how late it is?"

"Oh, I realize . . . ," Grassina grumbled, reaching for the bucket, "since you keep reminding me." Although she washed the first web by herself, she was afraid it would tear when she took it out. "Help me with this," she said, glancing at Chartreuse.

"Say *please*," her sister told her. "Princesses must never forget their manners."

"Please," Grassina said through gritted teeth.

"I don't see why you can't do it yourself," Chartreuse said as she helped carry the dripping web to the windowsill. After they'd draped it over the ledge, she shook her hands to dry them, splattering her sister with droplets. "I'm sure you can handle it from here. It shouldn't take you much longer, so I'll be off to bed now."

"We're supposed to do this together," said Grassina.

"We did. I have to go. I'm too tired to stay awake a minute longer."

"We've barely started . . . ," Grassina began.

"Good night, Grassina," Chartreuse said pointedly as she closed the door behind her.

Grassina reached into the pail for another web. The vinegar was cold and stung the little cuts she hadn't known she had, but she handled the webs as carefully as she could. It was very late when she realized that only a few remained in the pail. Even so, the castle wasn't completely silent. The sound of the guards making their rounds on the battlements carried through the still night air. The yowling of cats in the courtyard seemed extra loud and made Grassina feel edgy. She was relieved when a hound broke up the catfight.

When she'd laid out the last web to dry, Grassina tumbled into bed and fell asleep instantly. It seemed only a few minutes had passed before she woke to a voice screeching in her ear, "Get out of bed, you lazy lump!" Startled out of a deep sleep, Grassina lurched bolt upright with her heart trying to thud its way out of her chest.

Olivene stabbed her collarbone with one long, crooked finger. "It's almost dawn. Why are you lying around when you have work to do? I need you to find me a toad with seven warts."

"Can't I sleep a little longer?" Grassina asked, rubbing her eyes. "I was up most of the night washing the spiders' webs."

"No, you can't sleep! I need that toad now if I'm going to get my potion to work. Your sister is already on her way to her next chore. Why can't you be more like her? Get up and get busy!" Olivene waved her hand, using magic to tilt Grassina's bed so that it stood on end, dumping the girl and all her bedding onto the floor.

"Ow!" Grassina exclaimed. Untangling herself from her blankets, she glared at her mother. "You didn't have to do that! I was going to get up."

Olivene cackled and rubbed her knobby hands together. "I know! That's why it was so much fun." Turning to leave, she stomped out the open door, stopping only long enough to say, "Make your bed before you go anywhere. This room is a pigsty! Say, that gives me an idea—" Olivene pointed her finger at her daughter, but before she could do anything, Grassina had scrambled off the floor and slammed the door in her mother's face. The sound of hysterical laughter faded as Olivene walked away.

Grassina looked at her upended bed and bit her lip. It had been five days since her mother had become this awful creature, and every one of them had been terrible. Fortunately, Grassina had learned a lot since then, such as what she could and couldn't do around the queen. She knew better than to show fear in her mother's presence or to let her see that she was upset. It had surprised her to learn that standing up for herself was her best defense because it seemed to amuse her mother instead of making her angry. Chartreuse had yet to learn any of this, however, even though she'd spent the first day as a chicken.

It didn't help that Olivene had decided to make the girls assist with her magic, sending them on errands and giving them chores around the castle. Claiming that she didn't trust anyone but her own daughters to do the work, she'd had them collect milkweed pods in barrels, then made them take off their shoes and stockings, climb into the barrels, and stomp on the pods until the milky liquid squelched between their toes. Olivene had siphoned off the milk herself while sending the sisters to collect old snake skins from the woodpile and press them with hot irons, being careful not to damage the scales. Although they hated that job, it was less taxing than collecting the rainwater that puddled in the right footprint of left-handed people. That chore had taken most of one drizzly afternoon and had given both girls the sniffles. Not only had Olivene been unsympathetic, but she'd seen them returning to the castle and had immediately sent them to gather the dust under the benches on the western side of the Great Hall.

Grassina sighed. Finding the toad wouldn't be easy, but at least she could do it in the swamp, away from her mother's ever-watchful gaze. As she righted her bed and straightened the bedding, she wondered what chore her mother had devised for Chartreuse. A least they wouldn't be working together.

"Iss she gone?" whispered the little snake, whom Grassina had named Pippa. Complaining that she was cold, the snake had taken to sleeping under the blankets at the foot of Grassina's bed at night. Having a snake sleeping beside her feet had made Grassina nervous at first, but she and Pippa had soon grown used to each other. Each day after Grassina got out of bed, Pippa explored inside the castle walls, where she ate the mice that threatened to overrun the castle now that Queen Olivene was no longer maintaining her housekeeping spells.

Grassina had wrapped the snake's injured tail in a bandage, immobilizing it so it could heal. Because the tail was mending nicely, Grassina was already thinking about where she'd release Pippa when she was completely healed. Unfortunately, if the queen was going to make unannounced visits to Grassina's room, the chance that she might see the snake was something they couldn't risk.

"She's gone," Grassina said, feeling guilty that she hadn't done more to hide the snake. This was the first time her mother had visited the room since she'd changed, but Grassina was mad at herself for thinking that meant Olivene never would. Bending down, she picked up Pippa, saying, "You can't stay here any longer or Mother will see you. Who knows what she'd do to you then."

The little snake sighed. "It'ss my fault your mother actss the way she does. My bad luck changed her, and it keepss making her do awful things. You never should have brought me here. Don't missunderstand; I'm grateful for all you've done. You've given me a ssafe place to ssleep and all the fresh mice I can eat, but I jusst know you'd be better off without me."

"That isn't true!" said Grassina. "I told you before, I don't believe in your so-called bad luck. I'm sure that witch blamed you for all her problems because it was easier than blaming herself. If she'd patched her roof, or shut her door, or stayed awake, none of the bad things you mentioned would have happened. And as for my mother—my father would have brought her the flowers whether you were there or not. You had nothing to do with the curse. Now come with me and I'll take you somewhere safe where no one will bother you until your tail finishes healing."

"Will I be alone there? I don't want my bad luck to hurt any of your friendss."

"But I just told you . . ." Grassina shook her head and sighed. "Yes, you'll be alone, although I will come to see you as often as I can." With Pippa wrapped around her wrist, Grassina stroked the top of the little snake's head and wondered if there really was anywhere she could take her that would be truly safe.

Six

The guards had grown used to lowering the draw-bridge early in the morning so the princesses could do their mother's bidding, which made it easy for Grassina to smuggle Pippa out of the castle. What wasn't so easy was getting the little snake to stay hidden when she wanted to see everything that was going on around her.

Grassina had almost reached the drawbridge when Chartreuse called from the center of the courtyard. "Grassina! Wait for me!"

Although she considered pretending not to hear, Grassina knew Chartreuse wouldn't believe her. Sighing, Grassina stopped and turned, hoping she wouldn't have to wait long. Instead of hurrying, however, Chartreuse dawdled as if looking for someone, glancing back at the castle as she walked. Finally, a young man came through one of the doors. Chartreuse's face lit up, and she waved gaily when he looked her way. It was Prince Miguel, dressed for a morning ride.

While Grassina watched her sister smile coyly and laugh at something the young man said, Pippa poked her head out of the leather sack the princess was carrying. Grassina didn't look away from the flirting couple until she felt the little snake wiggle, making the sack thump against her hip. "What *are* you doing?" Grassina asked. "I told you to stay hidden."

Pippa peered up at her. "I wanted to know why we sstopped. It'ss imposssible to ssee anything from insside thiss sstuffy old bag, and the rockss in the bottom pinch my tail. I ssupposse it could be worsse though. With my luck it could have been filled with prickerss."

Grassina glanced at the closest guard. "Shh! Keep your head down," she whispered to the snake. "We stopped so we could wait for my sister."

"Really?" said Pippa. "I've never met your ssisster."

"And you're not going to, either. She'd probably scream and make a fuss, which is something I'd rather avoid."

"I bet she'ss like mosst humanss and doessn't like ssnakess."

"Lately, the only creatures she likes are handsome princes, so unless you're really an enchanted prince . . ."

Pippa sighed. "I'm not an enchanted anything, although I wish I were. Then maybe my luck would be better."

"Come along, Grassina," said Chartreuse, hurrying across the paving stones. "I don't have time to waste. Mother thinks I already left to start my chore, but I'd promised to have breakfast with the princes. If I finish the chore early enough, I'll be able to meet Prince Miguel in the garden when he comes back from his ride. Oh, look! There's Prince Clarence! Wait right here. I'll be just a moment."

"Not another one," said Grassina as her sister hurried toward a prince riding his destrier from the stable. Both the horse and the prince were dressed in armor, and neither one looked happy to be delayed.

"Where are you headed so early in the day, Clarence?" Chartreuse asked in her sweetest voice. "You didn't mention at breakfast that you were going anywhere."

"My squire told me that there's talk of a dragon in the woods only a few miles from the castle, dear princess," said Clarence. His highly polished armor reflected the morning sunlight directly into Grassina's eyes. She squinted, but didn't stop listening.

"Your squire must be mistaken," said Chartreuse. "No dragons would dare come so close."

"Perhaps, perhaps not," said Clarence. "But I feel it is my duty as your suitor to investigate the allegations and protect you if need be. Rest assured, sweet princess, if there is a dragon in those woods, I, Clarence, prince of the Mucking Peninsula and Outer Saltfort, will dispatch the monster so that it cannot possibly harm a single hair on your glorious head."

Chartreuse's eyes grew misty as she gazed up at him.

"Then ride, my champion, and take my token with you, knowing that I will await your return with bated breath."

"Could she be any more sappy?" Grassina muttered.

After searching her clothing for something that she could present to him, Chartreuse gave the prince a dazzling smile and said, "Just a moment." The prince waited while Chartreuse turned and ran to Grassina. "Quick!" she whispered. "You have a ribbon lacing the front of your tunic. Give it to me!"

"What?" squeaked Grassina. "Don't you have something you can give him?"

"No, and he doesn't have time to wait while I go to my room. Don't worry, I'll give you one of my ribbons later."

"This is so unfair," Grassina grumbled as she turned her back and unthreaded the pale green ribbon.

Chartreuse snatched the silky strip of fabric from her sister's hand and hurried to the prince's side. After pressing the ribbon to her lips, she tied it on his horse's bridle, saying, "Take this personal token of my high regard for you, my prince."

Clarence's armor clanked as he reached to touch the ribbon. "I shall carry it with pride, my princess."

"If it's my ribbon, is he my champion?" Grassina murmured.

"Why did she give your ribbon to that horsse?" asked Pippa, the tip of her nose peeking out of the leather sack.

"Shh!" whispered Grassina. "Here she comes."

"There you are, sister dear," said Chartreuse over the clopping of the destrier's hooves. Taking Grassina by the arm, she hustled her to the drawbridge, nodding when the guards greeted them. "I never realized that the boy cared so much for me," Chartreuse whispered when they'd passed by the men. "To think he'd be willing to give his life for my well-being. He must really love me!"

"Or love hunting dragons," Grassina said under her breath. Then she added in a louder voice, "Do you really think there aren't any dragons in the woods?"

"I'm sure I would have heard about it if there were. Since Mother lost interest in anything but her magic, I've been trying to stay informed about what's going on in the kingdom. When I'm the Green Witch, I'll be the one to deal with any problems. Unless Clarence goes deep into the enchanted forest, he's not likely to encounter anything more frightening than a bad-tempered squirrel. Now tell me, what does Mother want you to do? I have to collect blue butterflies, and I know just where to look. It shouldn't take me long, unless you keep dragging your feet."

"She wants me to get her a toad with seven warts."

Chartreuse looked shocked. "Is that all? That's not fair! She gave you the easy job."

"I thought you said you knew where to find blue butterflies," Grassina said, pulling her arm out of her sister's grasp. "Finding a specific toad will probably take a lot longer."

Chartreuse's expression brightened. "That's true. In that case, I'm glad I don't have that one!" After patting her sister on the back, she left her at the drawbridge to go her own way.

Pippa peeked out of the leather sack to watch Chartreuse. "How many princess want to marry her?"

"More than she can count," said Grassina. "A lot of princes want to marry a princess who'll be queen in her own right as well as a witch who could help their kingdom."

"There might be another reasson," said Pippa. "She might have shed her old sskin recently. Then she'd be nice and ssmooth. That might make her more attractive to maless."

Grassina laughed. "Maybe that's it. I'll have to ask her sometime."

Knowing that she didn't have long to take Pippa somewhere safe, Grassina decided to go to her tree house. It was on the way to the swamp—a perfect place to look for toads—and was unlikely to attract any other visitors.

When they approached the trunk of the tree that supported the miniature cottage, a squirrel chattered, "Go away!" Jerking its tail in anger, it skittered around to the other side of the tree when Grassina began to climb the ladder. Once inside the tiny house, the princess opened the sack and let the snake loose to explore. She'd brought a waterskin with her from the castle and used it now to fill a bowl for the snake. "It's just for a few days," she said, setting the bowl on the floor. "Your tail should be healed soon."

"It's nice and warm in here," said Pippa, raising her head to look around the room. She stopped when she saw the fireplace where the embers were still warm in the grate.

"That fireplace lights itself whenever the tree house gets cold," said Grassina.

"A ssnake could get ussed to this," Pippa said, slithering toward the hearth.

The copper finches twittered overhead while one of the few remaining glass birds rustled its transparent feathers, making them click softly. Pippa tested the air with her tongue, looking disappointed when the birds didn't smell real.

"You'll be safe here," said Grassina. "I have to go to the swamp to find a toad for my mother."

"Why? Doess she eat them?" the snake asked, her eyes glistening.

Grassina laughed and shook her head. "I have no idea what she plans to do with them, but at this point, nothing she does would surprise me."

"Doess anyone live here? Asside from the birdss, I mean."

"It used to be a playhouse for my sister and me," said Grassina. "No one comes here much anymore."

"Good," said Pippa. "Then my bad luck won't hurt anyone elsse."

Although Grassina had considered introducing Pippa to Marniekins, she decided that it might not be such a good idea. Pippa would probably fret about her bad luck more if she thought someone else might be hurt, and there was no way to tell how the doll would react to a snake.

Confident that her mother's old spell would keep Pippa safe inside the tree house, Grassina climbed down the ladder while clutching her toad-collecting sack. Starting at the base of the tree, she began lifting leaves and moving stems until she found a fat toad under a skunk-cabbage leaf near a mostly collapsed stone wall.

"Pardon me," Grassina said, picking up the toad to count the lumps on its back.

"What are you doing?" croaked the toad. "Put me down! This is so undignified! Why, I never . . ."

"I'm sorry," said Grassina. "I need to count your warts. These bumps are warts, aren't they? Mother told me to find a toad with seven warts, but I'm not sure these are what she meant."

The toad squirmed in her grasp and leaked something clear onto her fingers. "Ick!" she said. "What is that?"

"It's your own fault. You startled me. I can't help it if I have an incontinence problem when I'm startled. Now, if you wouldn't mind putting me down, we'll forget this whole thing ever happened and—"

"I can't put you down. Hold still so I can count your warts!"

"They're not warts! They're . . . uh . . . signs of age and wisdom. Yes, that's what they are. I'm not as young as I once was."

"Are you sure?" said Grassina. "They look like they could be called warts."

"Of course, I'm sure," said the toad. "It's my back, isn't it?"

Grassina sighed and crouched down, setting the toad back where she had found it. "There you go," said the toad. "That's right . . . put me on the nice soft moss and I'll . . . hop off as fast as I can!" The toad hopped wildly away from the skunk cabbage and into a crevice in the jumbled stones of the wall. "You won't catch me again. No, sirree! I'm safe in here, warts and all!"

"You little liar!" said Grassina. "I never should have believed you."

Resolving not to listen to any other toads no matter what they said, Grassina straightened her back and strode into the swamp, the empty sack swinging from her hand. It took some time before she found another toad, but it didn't have the right number of warts. Knowing that her mother would make her life miserable unless she returned with the desired toad, Grassina kept searching.

She found another toad in the short grass beside the edge of a pond, but it didn't have enough warts. A toad under the old willow had too many. All three toads that she found on the way to the northern edge of the swamp had too few. The sun was at its highest point when Grassina found the toad she needed. It was partially hidden under a rotting log, and she would have missed it if it hadn't made the dry leaves rustle when it moved.

Grassina bent down to peer under the log. The toad looked up at her and blinked. Before it could get away, she reached down and picked it up, counting the bumps on its back out loud. ". . . five, six, seven. You have seven warts. Finally! I was beginning to think I'd never find one like you."

"Now, isn't this just perfect!" said the toad. "As if my day isn't bad enough, a human has to come along and . . . Hey, what are you doing?"

Grassina carefully lowered the toad into the sack. "Taking you home with me," she replied, forgetting her resolution not to talk to the toads.

"Really? But we just met. Aren't you being a little presumptuous?"

"My mother needs someone like you," she said, peering into the bag.

"What for?" asked the toad.

"I'm not sure. She didn't say and I didn't ask."

"Is she a nice person or should I be worried?"

"She used to be very nice, but lately . . . Let's just say that she's not quite the same person anymore."

"In that case . . . ," said the toad, and with a giant leap, it flew out of the bag, hit Grassina squarely on the chin, and landed sprawling in the mud.

"Ow!" said Grassina. "Hey, come back here! I need you! My mother will turn me into something awful if I don't bring her a toad with seven warts!" As the toad hopped away, Grassina chased it, half bent over and nearly stumbling over the hem of her gown. She was still chasing the toad when she noticed the first paw print in the mud. It looked like it might belong to one of her father's hounds, only it was bigger and slightly longer. "That's odd," she said to herself.

Seeing another paw print a short distance from the first, she forgot about the still-hopping toad and knelt down to examine the prints. Grassina was familiar with nearly every kind of creature that had ever set paw in the swamp, yet this print was new to her. She went on, hoping to see which way the animal had gone, and stopped short. Another print was placed right where the creature's next step would have landed, yet it was different enough from the first that it could have been made by some other, perhaps larger, beast. The pads were longer and set farther apart. The print beyond that was also different, and the one beyond that was . . .

Grassina looked up at the sound of leaves rustling in the underbrush. It was a very little sound, yet it was loud in the still afternoon air. There was a smell as well—a musky kind of odor that was as unusual as the paw prints. Grassina shivered with the feeling that someone or something was watching her. Slipping her hand into the leather sack, she wrapped her fingers around one of her smooth, round throwing stones. She glanced at the prints again as she backed away. Whatever had made them was heading toward the enchanted forest. From the way the prints seemed to change with every step, Grassina was almost sure that it had come from there as well.

The rustling stopped as she backed away, but the sudden silence made her uneasy. Pulling the stone from her sack, Grassina took two more steps backward, then turned and started back the way she'd come, her ears straining to hear anything unusual behind her. The same sixth sense that had kept her safe so many other times had told her it was time to go home.

Grassina left the swamp and was passing the practice field when Chartreuse called out, "Grassina, is that you? Come over here and give me a hand!" Chartreuse tapped her toe with impatience until Grassina reached her side. Handing her younger sister the small wooden bucket she'd been carrying, Chartreuse said, "Mother is ruining my life! It didn't take me long to find those butterflies, but when I took them to her, she sent me out to pluck dandelion fluff. And I so wanted to talk to Prince Pietro. I told him how much I like poetry, and he was going to write me some. But look at what that fluff did to my fingers! No one will want to write poetry to my beauty after this." Still talking, she shoved pink fingertips under Grassina's nose. "It felt soft at first, but I've pulled so much of it that my fingers are worked nearly to the bone. It was bad enough that they were practically pickled in that vinegar last night. My hands are probably scarred for life. A princess shouldn't have to do things like this. It's a disgrace! I'm so tired, I could lie down right here and fall asleep—if the ground was cleaner. What have you been doing?"

"Looking for the toad I told you about," Grassina said, her face flushing as she remembered that she'd let the toad get away.

"And it took you all day? Just be glad you didn't have to pick dandelion fluff. My back is so sore from bending over that I feel like an old crone. Take that in to Mother for me," Chartreuse said, pointing at the bucket. "I need to wash before supper. I just hope I don't run into any of my princes before I change out of these dirty clothes."

Without the toad in her possession, the last thing Grassina wanted to do was go see her mother. "If that's what you want, but won't Mother think that I picked it all?" Swinging the bucket for emphasis, she raised it in such a big arc that the soft fibers threatened to fall out.

"Never mind!" Chartreuse said, snatching the bucket away. "I'll do it myself."

When they reached the castle, the two girls parted; Chartreuse went in search of their mother while Grassina headed for the dungeon. She knew she'd have to face her mother sometime, but she hoped to find another toad first. In the meantime, she wanted to talk to her father, the one person who could truly commiserate with her.

"I can't really talk to Chartreuse about it," she said from her seat on an old chest that her father had had carried down to the dungeon. Grassina was sitting in the room he'd taken over when Olivene decided that he'd been a rat long enough and changed him back into a human. It was a lot more comfortable than it had looked the first time she'd seen it; he'd had it cleaned out and a few pieces of furniture brought in, making it almost homelike. "When I try to talk to Chartreuse," Grassina continued, "everything is either about her or the kingdom. I don't think she cares about anything else. She can't see any of this from my point of view, or yours, and certainly not from Mother's. Although I suppose I can't blame her for that last part. Mother is terrible now. I know she hasn't been like this for long, but it's getting harder to remember her any other way."

"Not for me," said King Aldrid. "I can still close my eyes and picture her exactly the way she was the day we met. I started loving her that very first moment and never stopped, despite what she might have thought. It was my fault she became a victim of her family curse, and I'll never forgive myself. If only I'd listened to her mother."

"But you said that everyone thought Grandmother was crazy. I don't remember her very well, but I do remember that she did the strangest things. Once she had me stand with my feet in two buckets of water for most of an afternoon. She said she was trying to protect me from the fairies."

King Aldrid sighed. "That sounds like her. Maybe she knew something that we didn't. And now your mother . . ."

"Mother isn't crazy, she's cursed. There's a difference. A curse can be undone, and when I'm older, I intend to find out how. I want Mother back the way she was."

"We all do, sweetling," said the king. "Everyone that is, except your mother. She seems content with her new condition, although that might be part of the curse, too."

"She should be happy, since we're doing so much work for her," grumbled Grassina. "Even so, if we don't do exactly what she wants, she turns us into all sorts of things. I told you about being a rabbit. I was a mole yesterday morning. Chartreuse was a chicken for a few hours, but she won't admit to anything else."

"At least your lives are interesting," said the king.

Grassina laughed, but not because she thought it was funny. "Too interesting, if you ask me." Seeing a wistful expression on her father's face, she asked, "Is it that bad down here, Father?"

"I don't mind it," said her father. "I even like it in a way. My men come to see me, so I'm current with everything I need to do. And when I'm not working on the affairs of the kingdom, I've found time to write. I started creating a history of Greater Greensward years ago, but never had the time to finish it. I've been able to make some real headway the last few days because it's so quiet. I can't even hear the squabbling going on upstairs."

Grassina turned her head, unable to meet his eyes. She knew that at least part of the problem was the way she and Chartreuse couldn't get along. Even though she'd known that their arguing had disturbed their father, she'd never really tried to stop. And now that there seemed to be more than ever to argue about, she didn't see that it would ever end.

Grassina slid off the trunk. "It's getting late. I'd better go. But first," she said, remembering why she'd returned from the swamp, "I meant to tell you about something I saw today. There were paw prints . . . like a dog's or a wolf's, but very odd. They changed from one step to the next. I've never seen anything like it."

King Aldrid's gaze was sharp and direct. "How did they change?"

"The paw seemed to grow longer, the pads wider. . . . Why? Is it important?"

"I'm afraid so," said her father. "I was wondering when something like this would happen. I just wasn't expecting it so soon."

"Expecting what?" she asked.

"Paw prints like that belong to werewolves, my dear. It's a sign that things are about to go very wrong in Greater Greensward."

Seven

rassina got up early the next morning, borrowed a basket with a lid from a scullery maid, and made her way down to the swamp. This time she was going to be prepared; no toad would get away from her again. She had just set her wicker basket down and lifted the lid when something hurtled over the lip, making the wicker creak. "What was that?" she said, peering inside.

A surly-looking toad blinked up at her and said, "I'm a *who*, not a *what*. The least you can do is be nice to me, considering I put myself in here."

Grassina picked up the basket. "Why did you?" she asked, already counting the toad's seven warts.

"I don't rightly know," said the toad, sounding genuinely puzzled. "There I was, slurping up a worm, when all of a sudden my legs just carried me in. I'd jump out if I could, but my legs are locked up tighter than a snake's jaws on a muskrat. I don't suppose you'd want to take me out and set me back on the ground so I could finish my breakfast?"

"Not a chance," Grassina replied, closing the basket's lid. "You have seven warts, so you're just what I need. I'm not one to look a gift toad in the mouth."

"I never said I'd open my mouth so you could look in," said the toad, his voice muffled by the wicker. "You're awfully arrogant, thinking I would do that for you."

Grassina slid the little piece of wood to latch the lid. "I would like to know what compelled you to do it. Toads don't just jump into baskets for no reason. Something or someone," she said, looking around her, "*made* you do this. I wonder why."

"Because they're mean and ornery and hate me for no good reason that I can think of?" said the toad.

"Maybe . . . or maybe someone is trying to help me. Whoever you are," she said, raising her voice, "thank you!"

"Yeah," grumped the toad. "Thanks a lot!"

Pleased that she finally had the toad she'd been ordered to find, Grassina hurried to take it to her mother. She found the queen alone in the Great Hall, crouched on a bench while she pulled leeches off her dripping legs.

"That moat's full of leeches," said Olivene, glancing up at her daughter. "Good thing, too. Means I have a steady supply. A little boiled leech paste and . . . What is that you have there?" The queen's long nose quivered as she eyed Grassina's basket.

"It's that toad you asked for. I brought it as soon as—"

Olivene's lips pursed, and her eyes grew as cold as

iron. "I told you to get that toad yesterday! A day late is almost as bad as not at all. I think you need a little lesson about being slow, my girl."

The color drained from Grassina's face when her mother raised her arm. Setting the basket on the floor, she backed away, saying, "I'm truly sorry, Mother. It won't happen again! I've already learned my lesson."

"I'll be the judge of that," sneered Olivene. "Next time I'm sure you'll do whatever it takes to be prompt!"

‹❧›

The turtle skirted a moldy clump of tansy, shaking its head in disgust. The herbs that covered the floor of the Great Hall should have been replaced weeks ago, but ever since the queen had fallen prey to the family curse, a lot of things had been neglected in the castle. Two pages were just returning from watching the knights practice with swords and lances when one of them discovered the turtle. The freckle-faced boy, the son of a minor noble and the youngest page in the castle, stopped to poke the plodding turtle with his shoe. "Look at this! How do you suppose it got in here? Do you think it belongs to somebody?" The boy picked it up and flipped it over to examine its underside. Startled, the turtle pulled its head and limbs into its shell and squeezed its eyes shut.

A page with curly black hair rapped on the shell with his knuckles. With the authoritative air of someone a full year older, he said, "Nobody brings a turtle into the castle unless it's meant for supper. I love a good turtle soup."

"Maybe it escaped from the kitchen," said the first page. "Do you think Cook will give us a reward if we take it back?"

"Let's see if she has any tarts left from last night," the older boy said, reaching for the turtle. "Give it to me! I'll take it to her."

"And claim all the tarts for yourself? I don't think so!" Snatching his prize back, the younger boy took off running with his friend right behind.

Acting in a very unturtlelike manner, the captive stuck its head out of its shell, looking for a way to escape. Its head bounced painfully on its scrawny neck as the boy ran, but the turtle knew what would happen if it reached the kitchen: a little discomfort was the least of its worries.

"Cook!" shouted the page. "We found your turtle!"

"My what?" The head cook blinked sleepily at them from her seat by the fireplace, where she'd been dozing with a cat on her lap. She peered at the turtle as the pages held it up for her to inspect. "Ah," she murmured, "it's a nice turtle, too. Thank you, boys. I like a bowl of turtle soup now and then. Give it to Lettie there. She'll know what to do with it."

Thrusting its legs out of its shell, the turtle struggled to get down, but the boy held it away from his chest so that his captive had nothing to push against.

"Drop that right in this pot," said a chubby young woman with cheeks bright red from the cooking fire. "Oh, that's a good-sized one, that is! This water's cold, but it'll soon heat up over this nice hot fire, so . . . I say, what's this? Turtles aren't supposed to glow like that, are they?" The scullery maid was staring down into the pot with eyes as big as trenchers.

"What are you going on about, Lettie?" Cook said, dislodging the cat as she leaned forward in her seat.

"Agh!" shrieked the scullery maid. She dropped the pot, which had suddenly become too heavy to hold. It hit the floor with a clang, splashing water everywhere. While the maid backed away from the fire, the pages fought to see around her. They gasped when a person shot up out of the pot and went sprawling on the floor.

"Well, I never!" said Cook.

Grassina groaned and rubbed her head where she'd hit it on the edge of a table. Shaking her foot until it came unhooked from the pot handle, she sat up and looked around. "Sorry about the mess," she said, seeing the scullery maid's horrified expression.

Lettie gulped. "That's quite all right, Your Highness. Think nothing of it."

"Does this mean we won't get a tart?" the freckle-faced page whispered to his friend.

Grassina's cheeks were crimson as she hurried from the kitchen, leaving a trail of wet footprints behind her.

Avoiding the eyes of everyone she passed, she fled to her room, shivering in her damp clothes. It was the first time she'd had an audience when she changed back, and she felt oddly embarrassed. "I shouldn't worry about what other people think," she muttered, wriggling out of her clammy gown and into a clean one.

Grassina glanced out the window when she heard the rumble of thunder. The sky had darkened, and rain was already pattering on the sill. A breeze blew the dried plants that hung from her ceiling, making them rustle the way they had while alive. When the door flew open behind her, Grassina turned to see Chartreuse stalk into the room. "I heard what happened," said Chartreuse. "The whole castle is talking about it. What were you thinking of, turning back in front of so many people?"

Grassina flipped her braid over her shoulder. "I didn't have any choice. It wasn't as if I wanted to be a turtle or could choose when I turned back."

Sighing like someone carrying a great weight on her shoulders, Chartreuse flung herself on her sister's bed so that she was lying on her back with her arm covering her eyes. "It's bad enough that she likes turning us into things, but does she have to make it so obvious? My princes are bound to find out now, and I've tried so hard to keep it quiet. I've sent them on every errand I could think of just to keep them away from Mother. Clarence isn't back yet or I would have sent him, too. What's the point, though, if

Mother insists on making these spells so public? Someone is bound to tell my princes sooner or later. I'll never be able to live this down! Greater Greensward is going to be the laughingstock of all the kingdoms! On my way here, everyone stared at me as if I was about to turn into some awful creature. How could she do this to me?"

Chartreuse rolled over onto her stomach and stared accusingly at her sister. "Come to think of it, the entire thing must have been your fault. She turns us into horrid beasts when she wants to teach us a lesson, which means you did something to make her angry. What did you do this time?"

Grassina looked away and shrugged. "I was a little late bringing her the toad, that's all."

Chartreuse sat up abruptly. "I've nearly killed myself doing whatever she's asked me to do, but you couldn't bring her one stinking toad! Would it be too much for you to make a little effort to please the woman?"

The rain began to fall in grass-flattening sheets. A cackle of laughter as loud as thunder drew Grassina back to the window. She jumped when a jagged bolt of white light struck the ground at the edge of the moat, the boom so loud it made her ears ring. Wrinkling her nose at an acrid smell, she stepped closer to the window. The flash of lightning had shown her something so unbelievable that she had to look again to see if it was true. A figure dressed all in black was capering in the field below with her skirt hitched up and her skinny legs dancing across the lightning-singed ground. Her hair was flying as she twirled and spun, making snatching motions with her hands all the while.

"... if you would just think of others. Oh, for ..." Chartreuse hopped off the bed, grabbed Grassina's shoulder, and spun her around. "Have you heard a word I've been saying? I told you not to make a spectacle of yourself like that again! We're going to be the talk of the entire kingdom. No one will want to marry either of us!"

"I don't think they'll be thinking about us at all," said Grassina. "Not after they see what's going on outside."

"What are you talking about?" Chartreuse said, peering out the window. "There's nothing out there except ... Is that Mother? What is she doing in the rain?"

A bolt of lightning hit the ground, narrowly missing the prancing woman. Leaping into the air, she kicked her legs high and flailed her arms, then hunched over and slapped the ground. Although the girls had to clap their hands over their ears to still the ringing and make the thunder bearable each time another bolt struck, they were unable to look away from the cavorting queen.

"This is horrible!" Chartreuse shouted during a lull. The thunder had been so loud that everything else sounded muffled and distant. "We can't let anyone see her like that!"

"And what do you propose we do about it?" Grassina shouted back.

"We can . . . You should . . ." Chartreuse's voice trailed away as she tried to think. Then, nodding to herself, she declared, "We'll go see Father. He can talk to her."

"What can he do?"

"I don't know. He's her husband. She'll listen to him before she'll listen to us."

"Are you crazy?" Grassina asked, following her sister into the corridor. "You know what she's like now. She doesn't listen to anyone."

Chartreuse stopped long enough to glare at Grassina. "If you have a better idea, I'd be happy to hear it!"

Grassina swallowed and shook her head. For the first time in ages, Chartreuse actually wanted her suggestions. It was too bad that she didn't have any to give.

❦

Flickering torches lit the girls' path through the dungeon, making shadows jerk and waver around them. Because every surface was made of stone, every sound had its echo, with a hollow note that made even the most innocent noise seem sinister. Water seeping between cracks made the floor glisten and slippery to walk on and the air already sour with mold and decay smell even more pungent. One section of the corridor was so cold that Grassina could see her breath, yet there were no crosscurrents of air and there was no reason why it should be colder. Chartreuse shivered and hurried on, calling to Grassina when she lingered to look around. They were passing a cell with rusty bars in the tiny window when Grassina thought she heard voices; she peeked inside, but no one was there.

The only sign of life they encountered was a spider weaving its web across a doorway. "Listen!" said Grassina when she thought she heard something faint and far away and . . . Someone coughed and the sound echoed in the nearly silent hall. Following their ears to the door of their father's cell, they peeked inside and found him sitting hunched over a small table. "And to what do I owe this honor?" he said, having looked up from his quill and parchment when he heard the girls' hesitant knock.

"We've come to ask for your help," said Chartreuse. "Mother is dancing in the thunderstorm and making a spectacle of herself."

King Aldrid looked puzzled. "I'd like to help you girls, but I don't know what I can do about it. The queen has been avoiding me. We haven't spoken in days."

"I knew we shouldn't have asked him," Grassina blurted out. "He can't even leave the dungeon."

Chartreuse gave her father a pitying look. "Don't worry, Father. As soon as I come into my magic, I'll get you out of here."

King Aldrid cleared his throat. "That won't really be necessary. Your mother's spell kept me here for only three days. I could have left any time after that."

"Then why didn't you?" asked Grassina.

"To be honest, I've been avoiding your mother. As long as she doesn't see me, she leaves me alone. I've been able to handle the kingdom's business from down here, probably better than I could if I were upstairs running into Olivene. One flick of her finger and I'd be a rat again. Believe me when I say that no one wants a rat ruling the kingdom. If word got out that the king of Greater Greensward had been turned into an animal . . ."

"So what are we supposed to do about Mother? She has to be insane to do what she's doing!" said Chartreuse.

"She could get herself killed!" said Grassina.

"Your mother isn't insane. Just because she doesn't behave the way she used to doesn't mean that she doesn't know what she's doing," said the king. "I'm sure that whatever her reason is, it has something to do with her magic."

"But does she have to do it where everyone can see her?" wailed Chartreuse.

"She probably thinks it's more fun that way," said Grassina.

The king coughed behind his hand. "She probably does," he said, chuckling to himself.

Eight

Mwowr! screamed Chartreuse's kitten, slashing at the nose of the other cat. The larger honey-colored animal hissed and backed away, its ears flattened against its skull, its tail puffed out to twice its usual size.

Barking joyfully, a wandering hound took off after the cats, chasing them around the moat to the lowered drawbridge. A tinker stepped out of their way as the cats tore past. The kitten streaked over the gap in the boards, but the older cat missed its footing and slipped, falling through the gap and into the moat with a splash. As the kitten disappeared under the portcullis, the cat floundered in the water, its eyes frantic as it turned in circles, trying to find a way out. It might have made it had one of the larger fish that lived in the moat not come by and dragged it under the water. The cat yowled as it sank below the surface; then all that was left to show that it had been there were a few drifting bubbles.

Grassina stepped to the edge of the moat, clutching

her bucket of toadstools as she peered into the silt-laden depths. Then out of the water shot Chartreuse, spluttering and splashing, her streaming hair half covering her face. Blood mixed with water trickled from a scratch on her nose as she made her way to dry ground, paddling at first, then wading when her feet reached a rocky ledge.

"Need a hand?" Grassina asked, bending down to reach for her sister.

Chartreuse looked startled when she saw her and not at all pleased. "No," she said, her lips stiff as she climbed out of the water. "I don't need anyone's help, especially not yours. I hope you're happy. Rinaldo left at dawn this morning, and it was your fault. I just know he heard about your turtle incident."

Ignoring the gaping mouths of the farmers and merchants who had witnessed her misfortune, Chartreuse pushed her way through the usual morning crowd that had come to do business in the castle and limped across the drawbridge. Grassina saw her stiffen when Pietro passed under the portcullis, giving him only the briefest of nods. The prince turned as if to follow Chartreuse, but seemed to think better of it and continued across the drawbridge. Grassina shook her head when he stopped to talk to a group of farm girls carrying heavily laden baskets. She was watching the girls vie for his attention when her gaze fell upon a middle-aged man in homespun on the back of an old plow horse, its sides lathered from running too long and too fast. The man's face was pale despite his exertion, and his eyes had a hunted look.

The man was still astride his horse, arguing with the guards stationed at the end of the drawbridge, when Grassina approached them. "I'm telling you," one of the guards said to the man, "you can't see the queen. She's indisposed and won't see anyone."

"But it's important! A terrible thing has happened, and Queen Olivene needs to know. I have to talk to her."

"Perhaps I can help," said Grassina, stepping up to the guards.

Seeing the princess, the guards dipped their heads in deference, then swatted the man when he didn't do the same. " 'Tis Her Royal Highness Princess Grassina," said one of the guards. "Show some respect."

"Pardon, Your Highness," said the man, slipping off his horse and turning to Grassina. "My name is Hal of Darby-in-the-Woods. Dare I ask if you can help me? I must see the queen, yet these men tell me it isn't possible."

"What would you see her about?" asked Grassina. "I need to know if I'm to help."

The man shuddered as if what he had to say was too horrible for words. Glancing furtively at the guards, he inclined his head toward Grassina and whispered, "A pack of werewolves attacked my village last night. I came at first daylight. We need the help of the Green Witch. Three men are dead and two others were bitten, yet still live. We locked them in farmer Gib's shed, but who knows if it will hold when the change comes on them."

A sick feeling soured Grassina's stomach. "The guards were right, you can't see my mother now, but maybe I can talk to her for you."

"Would you?" Hal asked, hope displacing some of the fear in his eyes. "We're in sore need of her help. Frankly, we're surprised she hasn't come already, seeing that the Green Witch knows everything that goes on in Greater Greensward."

"Not everything," said Grassina. "And it's come as a surprise to us as well. I'll go see the queen, but I don't know if she'll help."

"Thank you, Your Highness," said the man. He looked so grateful that Grassina found it almost embarrassing.

❧

The day before, Olivene had moved her magical paraphernalia down into one of the cells, turning it into a workroom where she could concoct her potions and practice her spells. Grassina had yet to visit her there and had been putting off taking her mother the toadstools she'd demanded. Now, after promising the villager that she would talk to her mother, Grassina could no longer delay.

She thought at first that it might be hard to find her mother in the warren of rooms that made up the dungeon, but a thump, her mother's screech, and an even louder crash told her where to look. Grassina bit her lip, wondering what her mother had done this time. Following a loud tapping sound, she turned a corner where a damp fog smelling of rotting meat and skunk cabbage enveloped her. The fog was oozing out of the wall just outside her mother's door, growing thicker the longer she stood there. It was enough to make her eyes water, so she wiped them on her sleeve and tried to take shallow breaths as she took one step, then another. When the wall in front of her bulged and receded, she had to rub her eyes. Everything looked different from inside the fog. The ceiling seemed to shift above her, the floor rippled at her feet, and a window opened in a wall, then closed with a snap. Taking two quick steps, Grassina left the fog behind, and suddenly everything looked normal again.

Light flashed in staccato bursts from a doorway up ahead. "Oh, no, you don't!" shouted Queen Olivene. There was a thump and the light flashed brighter, then died down to a wavery, uneven glow. Steeling herself against whatever her mother might do, Grassina reached the door and peeked inside. Olivene was standing in front of a large cauldron, stirring its contents with a spoon as long as her arm. Each time the spoon made one full circuit of the pot, it hit the rim with a loud tap.

A book lay open on a table near the door. Grassina craned her neck to read the spell titled "Releasing Trapped Magic." She'd read only a few words when she smelled the fog again, so she stepped into the room to get out of its way and bumped into the table.

Olivene spun around and glared at her daughter. "What are you doing here? Don't just stand there staring like a gargoyle—come in and give me those toadstools." Before Grassina could move, Olivene had crossed the room and snatched the bucket from her hand. "Here," she said, thrusting the spoon at her. "Make yourself useful."

While her mother examined each toadstool individually, Grassina stirred the viscous liquid, wrinkling her nose at the frothy, hairy scum that floated on its surface. "There's something I need to tell you," she said.

"When I'm finished," her mother grumbled. Then she sniffed another toadstool.

Light flashing in the corner of the room made Grassina turn her head. A lidded wicker basket sat on the floor, isolated from the rest of Olivene's belongings. Tiny lights sparked through the gaps in the weave, like coals flaring in a dying fire. Suddenly, the basket fell on its side with a thump and began to roll. As it passed Olivene, she kicked it without looking up from what she was doing, sending it thudding into the wall. The basket buzzed angrily, then rolled back into the corner and flung itself upright.

"Let this be a lesson to you, girl," Olivene told Grassina. "Never collect insects in a thunderstorm expecting to get more effective lightning bugs. The darn things spark, but they don't have any real light. The crickets are the worst—it made them bad-tempered and smarter than they should be. Can't do a thing with them!"

"Why did you choose crickets?"

"Bugs are bugs, aren't they?" Glancing at the cauldron, Olivene said, "Watch what you're doing!" and pointed a crooked finger at the bubbling liquid. Grassina looked down to see it burble and ooze over the rim. "Hit it!" shouted Olivene. "Use the spoon and whap it hard!" Grassina whapped the concoction with the spoon, sending droplets flying. The liquid stilled, then slurped back into the cauldron.

"What's in this pot, anyway?" Grassina asked.

"None of your business!" Olivene snapped. Elbowing her daughter aside, the witch dropped in three carefully selected toadstools one at a time. When the third one was sucked in with a *glorp,* the liquid frothed as high as the rim of the pot before settling back down to a steady seethe.

Olivene's long nose quivered when she leaned over the pot and sniffed.

"I really need to tell you something," Grassina began.

Her mother held up her hand imperiously, saying, "Not now! Can't you see that I'm busy?" After another deep sniff, she dumped the rest of the toadstools into the pot, crowing with delight when it turned a sickly shade of blue. While Grassina retreated to the doorway, Olivene took a grisly-looking hook off the wall and dipped it into the pot, pulling out a dripping stocking.

"If you want something done right, you have to do it yourself," said Olivene, draping the stocking on a ring embedded in the wall. "That makes two pairs. Get a little potion on your clothes and suddenly no one wants to wash them for you. I was going to make you do it, but I decided that the wash water would work just fine as the base for my next potion. Hand me those leech lips and stand back. I should get a good reaction when I add them!"

Grassina studied the bottle labeled "Leech Lips." Some of the little, brown, squiggly things inside smacked themselves while others smiled or pouted. She told herself that it was the water's sloshing that made them move, but she wasn't so sure.

"I came to tell you that werewolves attacked a village last night," she said, handing the bottle to her mother.

Olivene's eyes brightened. "Really? Where?"

"Darby-in-the-Woods. A man came to see you about it."

"Did they kill any of the werewolves? Darby-in-the-Woods isn't far from here. I could be there and back in two shakes of a snake's tail."

"I don't think they did."

"Then why are you telling me about it? Unless some-one has collected a werewolf's whiskers or the last hair on the tip of its tail, I'm not interested." Uncorking the bottle, Grassina held it over the cauldron and shook out a few blubbering lips. The liquid seethed for just a moment, then became as placid as a lake in winter. "Drat!" muttered Olivene.

"You're the Green Witch," said Grassina. "It's your duty to protect the kingdom."

"Duty schmooty! Do you see a ring on this finger?" Olivene shoved her hand under her daughter's nose. "I'm no more the Green Witch than you are. If you don't mind, and even if you do, I have to get back to work. Now scat! I don't have time for all this tongue flapping."

"If you're not the Green Witch, then who's going to protect the kingdom? And what should I tell the man? I'm sure he's going to want . . ."

The basket filled with lightning bugs fell over with a *whump*—bursting open and letting all the bugs escape in a crawling, skittering, leaping, flying rush. "Now see what you've done?" shouted Olivene. "You've distracted me. It's going to take hours to catch those pesky pests, and I still haven't finished my laundry!"

"Maybe I could . . . ," Grassina began.

"Get out!" her mother shrieked, taking off her shoe and hurling it at her daughter.

Grassina darted from the room, ducking when the

second shoe sailed past her head. Olivene was still shouting at the insects as Grassina turned the corner, grateful that her mother had cast a shoe and not a spell.

"What's the ruckus about?" King Aldrid asked from an open doorway.

Grassina stopped and turned. She hadn't realized that her mother had claimed a room so close to her father's. "Did you know that Mother is no longer the Green Witch? It makes sense, of course. I mean, the Green Witch is the most powerful and the nicest witch in the kingdom, and no one can claim that Mother is nice anymore. But if she isn't, then who is? Do you think we should . . . Wait a minute. What's wrong with you?" She took a step closer, noting his sunken cheeks and the dark circles under his eyes. "You look awful!"

"It's good to see you, too," he said, giving her a weak smile.

"I didn't mean . . . I just . . . Are you all right?"

Her father had begun to cough so hard that he shook with the effort and had to look away until it was over. "I've seen better days," he wheezed when he could talk again. "Why did you come to see your mother? Is something wrong?"

Grassina nodded. "A man came to tell us that werewolves attacked people in his village!"

"And your mother doesn't intend to do anything about it, does she? Then I'd best see to it."

"You can't hunt werewolves. You're ill!"

King Aldrid shook his head. "There won't be any hunting involved. Werewolves turn back into their human form during the day, so my men and I will set traps and check them tomorrow. I was very adept at catching werewolves before I met your mother, but I haven't had to trap one since I moved to Greater Greensward. There was no need with the Green Witch watching over the kingdom. We were spoiled when your mother protected us, but now that she isn't doing that, we'll have to handle it ourselves the way rulers of other kingdoms do."

"But you should be resting."

"It's just a cold. I'll be fine. A little fresh air will do me good."

❧

Grassina was worried. She followed her father out of the dungeon, returning to her own chamber while he sent for the men he intended to take with him. She already had the necessary plants dried and hanging from her ceiling, so it didn't take long for her to mix a tonic for his cough. To her dismay, he and his men had already departed by the time she returned downstairs. With the tonic tucked safely in her purse, Grassina hurried to the stable and had her palfrey, Buttercup, saddled. Since she didn't know the way to Darby-in-the-Woods, she was glad that the head groom insisted on accompanying her. Normally, she would have chatted with the groom as they rode, discussing the weather, the crops in the fields they passed, and any unusual plants they happened to see, but she was so worried about her father that she couldn't think about anything else.

The sun was still climbing when they reached the point where the road to the village entered the forest. At first Buttercup seemed to enjoy the cooler air of the forest shade, pricking her ears and looking around with great curiosity, but after a time, she began to act nervous, startling at the smallest sound and snorting when the shade grew deeper. The groom's normally placid horse also seemed uneasy, prancing sideways when a squirrel ran in front of him. Buttercup shied at a dark spot on the road, fighting the reins until Grassina brought her under control.

They reached Darby-in-the-Woods without further incident just as her father and his men were riding out of the village in the opposite direction. Of all of Chartreuse's suitors, only Prince Limelyn had elected to accompany the king. The two royals rode side by side through the strangely quiet village, the single road dividing the cluster of cottages devoid of children, dogs, or geese to challenge a stranger's approach.

Here and there anxious faces peered from doorways, but no one came out to speak to Grassina as she passed by. A silent group of men stood in the shadow of the last cottage watching the king and his knights, turning their attention to Grassina only after Buttercup whinnied to the other

101

horses. One of the villagers, a tall man with long dark hair, stared at Grassina openly without any of the deference commoners usually paid to a princess. He made her feel so uneasy that she urged her horse to a gallop, joining her father in a shower of dust and pebbles.

"Grassina!" he said, turning his horse to face her. "What are you doing here?"

"Looking for you," she replied. "I brought you this." Reaching into her leather sack, she drew out the bottle of tonic and held it up for him to see. "It's for your cough."

"I appreciate your thoughtfulness, but that was neither necessary nor wise. These woods aren't safe if there are werewolves around."

"But you said that werewolves were active only at night."

"That isn't the point. Men from the village are already trying to track them down. Any hunters still out here will be using whatever means they can. It's during times like these that I particularly want you to stay close to the castle. Fear can make people do terrible things.

The king looked around, letting his eyes fall on two of his men. "Stay behind and see that we're not followed. There were no dogs in that village, which probably means that the werewolves have already disposed of them. Werewolves hate dogs because dogs hate werewolves and can find them when no one else can. I would have brought my own if I'd been thinking straight. No matter now. Just keep your eyes and ears open. Some of the villagers may have been turned into werewolves already and would be happy to see where we place our traps. And as for you," he said, looking at his daughter, "you'll have to stay with me now. We'll be returning to the castle as soon as we've dug some . . ." King Aldrid broke off when a deep, wracking cough made him close his eyes and grip his saddle to keep his balance.

Grassina watched with concern until her father's cough subsided. "Please try the tonic," she said, uncorking the bottle and handing it to him.

"Did you make this or did your mother?" he asked, sniffing it suspiciously.

"I did. It should help calm your cough."

"You're a very thoughtful girl," he said before taking a sip from the bottle. "Just like your mother used to be," he added, wiping his mouth with the back of his hand.

◦❧

No one spoke as they rode into the forest, leaving the village and the two knights behind. They hadn't gone far when a horse whinnied deeper in the woods. The party stopped to wait while Prince Limelyn and three knights rode off to investigate, returning with an armored destrier, its head hanging as it limped across the forest floor. "I think that's Clarence's horse," said Grassina. Even in the shade of the tall trees she could see that the armor of the riderless horse was no longer bright and shiny, but was smudged with something dark.

Slipping off her mare, Grassina ran to the destrier and reached for his bridle where a singed scrap of pale green ribbon still dangled. A smear of black came off on her finger. It was soot. As her father rode up, she raised her hand to show him. Rubbing her thumb and forefinger together, she said in a subdued voice, "I guess there really was a dragon after all."

With the destrier slowing them down, the knights didn't go far before stopping to lay the first trap—just far enough that no one from the village could hear them. While some of the men dug a deep hole, others cut down branches and saplings, whittling the ends to make sharpened stakes. Once King Aldrid declared the hole deep enough, one man was lowered in to line the bottom with the stakes, angling them upward so they'd impale anything that fell in. When he was finished, they rode on to the next likely spot, leaving two more men behind to cover the hole and erase any sign of the trap.

"How do you know where to put them?" Grassina asked her father when they'd stopped once again.

"We dig the traps near the road where a werewolf might lie in wait for an unsuspecting traveler. Werewolves are stronger and faster than either men or wolves. They have the wolves' fangs and a man's intelligence, yet they avoid fair fights whenever possible. For all their nasty, brutish ways, werewolves are basically cowards. They hide from their prey where the wind will carry their scent away, sneaking up when they are sure to take them by surprise. Only stout locks and tall trees will keep them at bay, because they can neither manipulate locks with their paws nor climb higher than they can jump."

Grassina shuddered as she peered into the deeper gloom of the forest. "What should I do if I see a werewolf?"

"Just stay in the castle," said her father. "It's the only place you'll be truly safe, especially if there are dragons around as well."

Nine

Grassina was still in bed the next morning when a buzzard smelling of its recent meal of rotting muskrat flew in through her window and dropped a note on her. "She was right," said the bird as it landed on the sill. "Although why anyone would be in bed this late in the day is beyond me."

Rolling over, Grassina blinked, then sat up with a start when she saw the filthy bird. The buzzard snickered at the frightened look in her eyes, clacking its beak in irritation when the note fluttered off Grassina and onto the floor.

"Don't just sit there," said the buzzard. "Pick it up and read it! Why do you think I'm here? She said you were slow as well as lazy and that I should lend you a wing if you needed it." Extending a wing covered with dried blood and reeking bits of offal, the bird snickered again when Grassina retreated to the far side of the bed. "She said you'd be prissy. You might as well get the note though. I'm not leaving until you do."

Keeping her distance from the bird, Grassina slipped out from under her covers and knelt on the floor, reaching under the bed for the wayward note. "Good," said the buzzard. "It's officially delivered, so I'm off. I'd read it right away if I were you. You don't have much time since you've already slept away most of the morning."

Grassina glanced out the window as one of the castle's roosters crowed. The sun was just rising over the tops of the trees in the distance, and the first rays had yet to reach the cold stone walls. The buzzard flapped its wings and flew away, shedding a loose feather that drifted onto Grassina's bed. She didn't notice, however, because she was already trying to decipher her mother's handwriting.

Grassina,

Get your lazy rump out of bed and go to your precious swamp. Find enough eggshells from just-hatched blackbirds to fill a washtub and bring them back to me before midnight tonight. If you fail to do this, go straight to the moat and make yourself comfortable, because I'll be turning you into a slimy, loathsome snail.

Signed,
Queen Olivene (your mother)

P.S. Have Cook bring me some rotten grapes, stale bread, and a flagon of brackish water. Yesterday's breakfast was so good I can't wait to taste it again.

107

"How am I supposed to do that?" Grassina muttered, thinking about the size of the washtubs she'd seen in the kitchen. The task was so daunting that she was tempted to give up before she'd even begun, but she couldn't—not if she didn't want to become a snail for who knew how long.

This time when Grassina sought out a scullery maid, she asked for the smallest washtub. Unfortunately, even the smallest tub was unwieldy when the princess tried to carry it herself. Grassina staggered under its weight as she lifted it with both arms and lugged it out of the castle and across the drawbridge. She had to set it down twice so she could rest before reaching the tree house, groaning each time she picked it up.

Grassina was setting the washtub down once again when she thought about Pippa. It had been days since she had last visited the little snake, but she'd been so busy, she hadn't had a chance. Grassina bit her lip. She hadn't taken Pippa any food in all that time either, and with the queen's magic keeping the snake inside . . .

Something crunched under her feet as Grassina approached the ladder. Broken glass sparkled on the ground, some of it still in the shape of feathers. Worried, Grassina hurried to the ladder and began to climb, almost falling when a rung snapped beneath her foot. She gripped the ladder with white-knuckled hands, her heart racing. After that she tested each rung before putting her weight on it and was relieved when she reached the platform. Her relief gave way to dismay when she saw the cottage. Wasps buzzed through the open window. Branches from the supporting tree had broken, smashing through the roof and some of the platform boards.

"It's like the castle," murmured Grassina. "When Mother changed, she stopped caring about a lot of things. She must have let the maintenance spells lapse." Stepping over the larger debris, she set her hand on the door, which was sagging so badly that she had to give it a hard shove to move it out of her way.

More shards of glass littered the floor inside, and the copper birds were gone. The fire was out in the fireplace, where even the ashes were cold.

"Pippa!" called Grassina. "Are you here?"

At first there was no reply, but then over the creaking of the tree's branches and the angry complaint of the wasps, Grassina heard a faint, almost tentative tapping coming from the wooden trunk in the corner. Skirting a branch that protruded through the ceiling, she reached the trunk and lifted the lid. Hector's eyes were wild when he whinnied to her, but Marniekins looked even worse. Her dress was disheveled, her wool hair a stiff corona around her head. The poor doll was so upset that she couldn't stop wringing her hands.

"Oh, Princess, I'm glad you came!" exclaimed the doll. "There was a big storm and the wind shook our tree and there was crashing and banging and it was just awful!"

"Are you all right?" asked Grassina.

Marniekins nodded until Grassina feared that her head would come off. "We're fine. We stayed in the trunk while your friend told us what was happening. Pippa was so nice! She talked to me after you left and told me about monkeys and bright-colored birds and scary lizards and all sorts of things. But then the storm came and everything changed and she left to get something to eat and never came back."

Grassina frowned, wishing she had come sooner. "I hope she wasn't hurt. She already had an injured tail."

"She told us about that," said Marniekins. "She told us about how she met you, too. Were you really a rabbit?"

"Yes," said Grassina, scooping up the doll and tucking her in her sack. "And I'll be something else if I don't find the eggshells my mother wants. I'm taking you and Hector with me. You can't stay here any longer."

"Where are we going?"

"After I do something for my mother, I'll have to hide you in the castle. Rag dolls and wooden horses don't last long outside in bad weather."

"But didn't you take Pippa out of the castle because it wasn't safe?"

Grassina nodded. "That's true. But this time I don't have any choice."

As the swamp wasn't far from the tree house, Grassina forced herself to carry the washtub without stopping once. She sighed when she finally set it down by a pond.

"This is a beautiful place," Marniekins said, peeking out of Grassina's leather sack. "But what kind of errand would your mother send you on that would bring you here?"

"I have to collect enough blackbird eggshells to fill this tub. If I don't, she'll turn me into a snail and I'll have to live in the moat."

"That's so mean! I saw your mother only a few times, but she didn't seem mean to me."

"Mother wasn't horrid until recently. A curse turned her nasty. Now she orders us around and makes us get her all sorts of strange things."

"And if you don't get them, she turns you into a snail?"

"Not always. She turned me into a turtle yesterday. And when I met Pippa, I was a rabbit, remember?" Grassina sighed. "I don't know how I'll ever find the eggshells, let alone enough to fill this tub, so I'll probably be a snail before the day is out."

A sound like muffled thunder made Grassina look up. An angry-looking cloud was forming over the trees to the north. As it grew, it seemed to writhe and churn, becoming darker and more ominous each moment. With a muffled shriek, Marniekins pulled her head into the sack and tugged it closed behind her.

When Grassina finally realized that the cloud was

coming her way, there wasn't time to reach shelter. She was looking up into the heart of the cloud when it started to break apart, raining bits of itself down on her. Crouching low to the ground, she covered her head with her arms, squeezed her eyes shut, and waited for whatever it was to strike. A roaring wind nearly knocked her over, carrying with it a pungent odor. The sound grew so loud, it was deafening, yet Grassina remained untouched. Warily opening her eyes, she was surprised to see blackbirds hurtling past, one after another, slowing long enough to drop something from their beaks into the washtub. Having decided that the birds weren't coming after her, Grassina sat back on her heels to watch the cloud lessen and finally disperse. When the sky was clear once again, she peered into the washtub and was surprised to see that it was filled with bits of broken eggshells.

"The blackbirds brought me the eggshells I needed!" Grassina exclaimed. "I wonder who did this." Turning her head from side to side, she tried to spot her mysterious benefactor. "Those birds wouldn't have done it on their own. It's just like when the toad jumped in the basket. Someone with magic must be doing this. A fairy perhaps . . . Maybe even the swamp fairy. Hello! Whoever you are—thank you for your help!"

When no one appeared, Grassina picked up the tub, staggering under its even greater weight. The way back seemed longer than the trip out had been, and she had to set the tub down five or six times before she had the castle in sight. Whatever magic had made the birds bring her their shells hadn't made the tub or its contents any lighter.

Grassina had passed the practice field and could smell the fetid water of the moat when she heard a woman screaming. An anguished, wavering cry of loss and despair, the sound would have made her turn and run if it hadn't been coming from the castle. Dropping the washtub with a loud thump, she ran toward the drawbridge. Her first thought was that the werewolves had somehow gotten past the defenses, but she couldn't understand how it could have happened. The moat completely encircled the castle, and the drawbridge was always well guarded. Only something with wings could have gotten over the castle walls, and even then . . .

A piercing shriek made Grassina stumble and nearly fall. The sound dissolved into a wordless wail that clutched at her heart and brought involuntary tears to her eyes. She looked up when a woman wearing a long, white gown drifted through a tower window, wailing and tearing at her streaming white hair. The woman swooped low enough that Grassina could see her bloodred eyes and gaunt features. "Woe is me!" the woman wailed. "Death and destruction shall visit this castle before the day is out!"

As the woman flew off, heading north toward the

enchanted forest, a feeling of absolute desolation swept over Grassina, leaving her feeling lonely and bereft. The guards on the battlements, the farmers delivering chickens, and the pages chucking stones into the moat were frozen in place as if the wail had the same power to render them as immobile as the frigid north wind.

When the cries of the woman had faded away, Grassina was once again able to move, although with a dragging step and a heart that ached with unnamed sorrow. The faces of the guards stationed by the drawbridge were pale, their expressions stricken. Grassina tried not to look at them too long, knowing that their faces mirrored her own and only made her sorrow harder to bear.

Her feet seemed to move of their own volition, carrying her across the open courtyard into the castle, where the sound of crying seemed natural after the heart-rending wail. She found Chartreuse huddled on a bench in the Great Hall, sobbing. Prince Limelyn was sitting beside her holding her hand while Torrance sat on the other side with his arm around her shoulder. The other princes stood at the far end of the table, looking uncomfortable.

Prince Limelyn jumped to his feet when he saw Grassina, relinquishing his seat for her. "What happened?" she asked, putting her arms around her sister.

"The banshee...," Chartreuse cried. "She flew through the castle, screaming and tearing out her hair and frightening everyone and saying that . . . that . . . Oh, Grassina, it's too awful! Father is going to die today!"

"I don't believe it, unless . . ." Grassina narrowed her eyes in suspicion. "Did the banshee do something to Father?"

Chartreuse shook her head, making her honey gold curls fly. "I don't think she went near him, but then, she wouldn't have to. She's a banshee! They always know when someone is going to die."

"Have you gone to see Father? I hope he didn't hear this nonsense. Nobody in this castle is going to die today!"

"I told you . . . banshees know these things."

"Well, this time she's wrong," said Grassina, helping her sister to her feet. "Now stop crying. We'll go visit Father and you'll see that he's all right."

Nearly a dozen people stopped them in the hall as they headed to the door at the top of the dungeon stairs, and they all wanted to offer their condolences. "We're so sorry to hear about your father," some said.

"He was the best king we've ever had," said others.

"Our father is fine," Grassina said each time while Chartreuse cried harder.

Chartreuse was sobbing loudly again when they closed the dungeon door behind them and started down the stairs, but even she noticed that the shadows seemed to draw closer the louder she cried. It frightened her enough that she straightened her shoulders, gave a few last shuddering sobs, and wiped her eyes with the tips of her fingers.

The sisters had almost reached their father's room when Olivene popped through the doorway and glared at them. "Where do you think you're going?" snapped the queen.

"To see Father," said Grassina. "We wanted to make sure he was all right."

"Well, he's not," Olivene said, so angry that her voice shook. "Fine daughters you are, coming to see him only after he's dead."

Grassina shook her head. "No, you're wrong. Father can't be dead. I saw him yesterday. He said he had a cold."

"He's deader than a doornail and there's nothing you can do about it, so go away and leave us alone."

"Father is dead!" wailed Chartreuse. "The banshee was right! I told you, Grassina, but you wouldn't listen!"

Grassina was too stunned to reply. She felt as if the floor of the dungeon had dropped out from under her and she was falling into an abyss. Her father was gone. The only person who understood her, the only person who she knew really loved her, was gone. "Can we see him?" she whispered, her throat feeling tight and prickly.

"No, you can't see him. I was saying my good-byes, so go away! I wasn't finished."

While the girls watched, stunned, Olivene scuttled back into the room and slammed the door. Tears trickled down Grassina's cheeks as she took her older sister's hand in hers. "We'll come back later, after she's finished saying good-bye."

Something made of glass hit the door on the other side, shattering. "You're a no-good, rotten liar!" screamed the queen.

Chartreuse nodded. "Maybe she'll go upstairs soon."

There was a thud, and the door shook. "How dare you leave me?" screamed Olivene. "I was supposed to go first! It wasn't supposed to be like this."

Chartreuse glanced back at the door as her sister led her away. "Mother doesn't grieve like everyone else," said Grassina.

"I know," said Chartreuse. "But then, Mother doesn't do anything like anyone else."

❧

Once upstairs, Chartreuse left Grassina, saying that she wanted to be alone. Grassina felt numb and empty as she slipped away to her chamber. The loss of her mother to the family curse had been a blow, but nothing like this. At least then the girls had still had one normal parent who cared about them. Now all they had was their mother, a horrible person who cared only for herself.

Grassina stayed in her room until late afternoon, when she heard a commotion outside. Wiping the tears from her eyes, she took a shuddering breath and went to her window. Chartreuse and Prince Pietro were walking toward a crowd gathered around a man who was waving his arms and gesturing. When he turned his head to look at the castle, Grassina saw that it was her father's gamekeeper, Milo Blum, a normally quiet and sedate man.

After splashing cold water on her face, Grassina hurried down the stairs. Chartreuse was already there talking to Milo when she arrived. Prince Pietro was lingering only a short distance away, looking irritated.

"I went to see for myself," said Milo. "The stream is poisoned. A Vila probably did it, just like the one in Upper Montevista three years ago."

"Isn't there anything you can do about it?" asked Chartreuse.

Milo Blum shook his head. "I don't know. We've never had a Vila in Greater Greensward before. I don't even know what to look for or how to track her."

"What is a Vila?" asked Grassina, stepping through the crowd.

"I've heard she looks like an incredibly beautiful young woman dressed in white. She lives in the woods and protects the animals. They say that Vili don't like hunters and poison the streams they drink from to keep them from coming back. What with the werewolves ... and now the Vila ... no one wants to go into the forest anymore. I told Cook that's why I won't be bringing her fresh meat for tonight's supper."

Chartreuse silenced him with another wave of her hand. "Thank you for telling us. Please keep us informed of anything else you hear. That will be all for now."

"Yes, Your Majesty," Milo said, bowing to her as if she were the queen. It struck Grassina that Chartreuse was more of a queen than their mother, at least the way their mother was now.

"So what should we do?" Grassina asked her sister as they crossed the courtyard together. "Do you think we should assemble the knights and ask for volunteers to find the Vila?"

"No," said Chartreuse. "The Green Witch has protected this kingdom for hundreds of years, but Mother doesn't care what happens to Greater Greensward now. I'm sure Father could have handled it, if he were still . . ." When her eyes started to well with tears, Chartreuse took a deep breath and blinked furiously for a moment. After clearing her throat, she added, "I may not be the Green Witch yet, but I will be someday, so I guess this is going to be up to me."

"What can you do?" asked Grassina. "You're only fifteen and don't have a speck of magic."

Chartreuse lifted her chin. "I'm going to have magic," she said, sounding defiant. "It just hasn't shown itself yet. Maybe this is what it will take to get it started. I'll go down to Mother's workroom and look through her books. I'm sure she'll have some kind of spell I can use."

"Do you really think she'll let you look at them?"

"I wasn't going to ask her! I'll just slip in when she comes up from the dungeon. Leave it to me," said Chartreuse. "I know what I'm doing."

"Then I'm going with you," said Grassina. "Two pairs of eyes are better than one."

⚮

Hiding in the shelter of a nearby alcove, the girls watched the door to the dungeon stairs until their mother came into view. When she disappeared down the corridor, they slipped through the door and headed to her workroom.

"I want to see Father first," said Grassina, continuing down the hall past their mother's room.

Chartreuse stopped. "We may not have much time."

"We have time for this," Grassina said, placing her hand on their father's door. Although it felt like rough-hewn wood, the door was as unyielding as the stone around it. "It won't open," she said, pushing against it with both hands.

"Mother probably put a spell on it," said Chartreuse. "I hope she hasn't locked her workroom, too."

When their mother's workroom door opened easily, Chartreuse and Grassina slipped inside. A pallid pair of witches' lights glowed in the corner, bobbing against the ceiling like corks on a fishing line. They gave off a bluish light that made everything stand out in sharp relief, showing every line and freckle on the girls' faces.

While Chartreuse looked for the books, Grassina circled the room, examining everything that she hadn't dared approach when her mother was present. Dust-choked spiderwebs hung like lacework from the ceiling, swaying in a faint current of air. The skull of a griffin was mounted on the wall, its eyes still intact. When Grassina walked past it, she could have sworn the skull's gaze moved with her.

She had just found the basket containing the lightning bugs when something brushed against her ankles. Startled, Grassina looked down. Chartreuse's kitten was rubbing against her leg, purring so hard that its little body vibrated. "What's he doing here?" Grassina asked. "Did he follow us down the stairs?"

Chartreuse glanced at the kitten, then turned away. "I gave him to Mother. He wasn't nearly as sweet when I got to know him. I thought he and Mother would suit each other very well. They're both mean and self-centered. She's already named him Herald. Oh, good. Here they are!" said Chartreuse, standing in front of the only table in the room. A small stack of books was lying on it beside a tankard filled with a thick green liquid smelling strongly of week-old fish. "There aren't very many. I always thought she had more than this. That's good, I guess.

It won't take long to look through them. Listen, this spell is for . . ." Chartreuse had flipped to the front page and was reading the very first words when the book flew up into the air, closed itself, slapped her hands, and landed on the table. "Did you see that?" she asked with a squeak in her voice.

"Maybe you did something wrong," said Grassina. "Try another book."

Chartreuse gingerly opened the next book. "This one seems all right. It says . . ." This time when she began reading, the book flew up, fanned its pages in her face, pinched her nose, and fell back to the table, closed once again.

"I don't think they want you to read them," said Grassina.

"I don't believe this!" said Chartreuse, rubbing her nose. "No stupid book is going to do that to me!" This time the book struggled when she picked it up, but she held on tight with both hands and forced the book open. With an angry shriek, the book shouted, "Robber! Scoundrel! Set me down, you no-good book thief!" and wiggled out of her grasp. Once free, the book began to hit her until she backed away, waving her hands to fend it off.

"What's going on in here?" demanded a voice by the door. Both girls turned to face their mother, their eyes wide in dismay. Chartreuse flinched when the book gave her another solid whack.

"Were you fiddling around with my books?" demanded Queen Olivene.

"Me? No, of course not!" protested Chartreuse. "I wouldn't touch anything of yours."

"Liar!" shouted the book.

"Liar! Liar!" echoed the rest of the books on the table.

"You lied! You know what I do to liars, don't you?" Olivene asked with a malicious gleam in her eyes.

Chartreuse backed away from the table. "I wouldn't touch your crummy books! They probably wouldn't have what I need anyway."

"Hypocrite!" screamed all the books at once as they rose up and began to flap their pages at her.

Olivene chortled gleefully, rubbing her hands as her older daughter tried to dodge the books. Horrified, Grassina looked around for something she could use to stop their assault. Her eyes settled on the basket of lightning bugs, agitated now by all the noise. Although the sound coming from the basket had been little more than a soft hum when the girls first entered the room, it had risen in volume until it was almost as loud as the books, and sparks were shooting out of the holes in the weave.

"Mother, make them stop!" screamed Chartreuse as the books continued to assail her.

"It's your own fault," Olivene shouted over the din. "You're getting exactly what you deserve!"

"Then I'll stop it," Grassina said under her breath as

she kicked the lightning-bug basket as hard as she could. The basket careened into the wall, splintering the brittle wicker and freeing all the bugs. Suddenly, they were everywhere—crawling, flying, skittering, hopping, and inching their way across the room. Although Grassina ducked away from the flying insects, they flew past her in a swarm that twinkled like stars, knocking over bottles, books, and anything else that stood between them and the queen.

Olivene screamed when the first wave hit, shocking her with their wings, their legs, their bodies. She started hopping around on one foot, then the other as the crawling bugs reached her. Grabbing her sister's hand, Grassina pulled her out of the room and into the corridor where the girls threw their arms around each other, laughing.

Ten

"I'm not going back down there!" Chartreuse cried later that night. "It's a horrible place. I don't ever want to set foot in there again."

Grassina patted her sister's arm. "It's all right. I'll go by myself. I want to see if the door to Father's room is still locked. We'll have to arrange for his funeral tomorrow, but I wanted to see him first."

Chartreuse glared at her sister. "If you're trying to make me feel guilty, it's not going to work. I loved him, too, you know."

"I'm not *trying* to do anything. Mother went out, so I came to see if you wanted to go with me. Since you don't . . ." Grassina shrugged. She didn't really want to go by herself, but she would if it was the only way.

Chartreuse sputtered. "You're going down there? By yourself? At *night*? That's the stupidest thing I've ever heard!"

Grassina slipped off the edge of her sister's bed and

started for the door. "I'm sorry I woke you. I didn't want to wait any longer to see him, and I thought you'd want to go, too. Go back to sleep and I'll see you in the—"

Throwing back the covers, Chartreuse shot Grassina a nasty look. "Oh, stop being the martyr. You know I can't let you go by yourself. I'd never forgive myself if something happened to you, too. Just give me a few minutes to get dressed and we'll go to the lousy dungeon. I must be crazy to do this," she muttered, reaching for her tunic. "That is the absolute last place I want to go at night."

"I don't understand why," said Grassina. "There's nothing down there that can hurt us."

"Oh yes, there is," said Chartreuse. "Mother!"

༺๛༻

Although it was always dark in the dungeon, it seemed even darker at night. There were only a few small windows to let in a breath of air, and none where the girls were going, yet the dungeon *felt* different than it did during the day. A sense of silent waiting pervaded the air as if the dungeon knew that something was about to happen. As neither of the girls wanted to see what that something might be, they hurried down the corridor, slowing to a quiet tiptoe only when they passed the door to their mother's workroom.

This time when they tried their father's door, it wasn't locked. The girls slowly pushed the door open, and

Grassina held up the torch she'd carried with her. Except for broken furniture and torn bits of parchment littering the floor, the room was empty.

"Where's Father?" said Grassina, peering into the corners.

"You think I keep dead bodies around here, cluttering up the place, just so people can come and gawk?" said their mother from the doorway.

Grassina turned slowly to face her. "I thought you'd gone out."

Olivene chortled. "Obviously—or else you wouldn't be here. Well, I'm here and he's not. I had him buried hours ago."

"Without letting us say good-bye?" cried Chartreuse.

"I said good-bye for you. And now I'm saying good-bye *to* you. Good-bye. Go away. I want my peace and quiet."

The girls slunk out of the room under their mother's gaze. They hadn't gone far when they stepped into the fog. It had grown since Grassina had seen it last, and it smelled even worse than before.

"What is that stench?" asked Chartreuse, wrinkling her nose.

"I think it's magic Mother released from the walls. At least I saw it coming out of the wall earlier, and I saw a spell for releasing magic in Mother's workroom."

"You saw a spell for releasing magic and didn't tell me?

Don't you see, that might work on me!" In her excitement, Chartreuse turned around and was about to go back when Grassina stopped her.

"What are you going to do, ask Mother for the book?" said Grassina.

Chartreuse shuddered. "You're right. Never mind. It probably wouldn't work on a person anyway. And if it did, it probably wouldn't do me any good, not if it was one of Mother's spells." She stopped talking to peer into the darkness that seemed to move just beyond the light of the torch. "What is that? Is someone there?"

Grassina looked in the direction her sister was pointing. "It's probably this fog. It makes things look different."

"Maybe so, but it looks so real, almost as if—"

"I may not know a lot about courtly manners, but it seems to me that pointing is rude," said a wavering voice. "Who do you think you are, chit, pointing at me that way?"

"Now Hubert," said a younger and steadier voice, "I'm sure the girl didn't mean any harm by it."

"Who are *you*?" demanded Chartreuse, looking at the two approaching figures. "Are you blind that you can't see to whom you're speaking? I'm Princess Chartreuse and this is my sister, Princess Grassina. I expect, no, I demand an apology this . . ."

Chartreuse's voice faded away as Hubert and his companion drew closer. It wasn't so much the way the old, stooped figure in the tattered tunic and his younger, well-dressed companion walked that drew her eye as the way they weren't walking at all. Both men appeared to be floating a few feet above the ground, which was convenient since neither one seemed to have any legs below their knees. The rest of their bodies began to materialize as she watched, open-mouthed, although they remained slightly transparent.

"Are you . . . Can you be . . . Is it possible . . . ," stammered Chartreuse.

"They must be ghosts," Grassina whispered in her sister's ear.

"Ghosts?" Chartreuse said, the word ending in a squeak.

"Pardon me, Your Highness," said the younger figure. "I'm Sir Jarvis, and this is my friend Hubert. At your service." With a polished gesture, the ghost whipped off his pointed cap and bowed deeply. Chartreuse gasped when his head fell off and rolled across the floor.

The head came to a stop faceup, but its lips had collected dirt as it rolled. "Pleh! Pleh!" Sir Jarvis spit, then rubbed his lips together and said, "I'm so sorry, Your Highness. There are still times I forget that I'm not all one piece."

Chartreuse's voice reached a higher octave when the headless body began patting the ground with its right hand. She swayed when its right arm dropped off.

"Don't lose your head, Jarvis," said Hubert. The hand

on Sir Jarvis's unattached arm was still patting the ground when Hubert picked up the head and set it back on his friend's neck.

"Ah, there we are," Sir Jarvis said, reaching with his remaining arm for the one on the floor. "It's been more than two hundred years since I was drawn and quartered, but one tends to forget such things."

Chartreuse swayed once and collapsed, lying sprawled on the cold stone floor.

Sir Jarvis was still talking when he shoved his arm bone into the socket. "I apologize for . . . Oh dear, I believe the young lady has fainted."

Grassina dropped to her knees. "Chartreuse! Are you all right?"

"I think we should go," Sir Jarvis told Hubert. "There's nothing we can do, and no one wants to be in such an embarrassing position around strangers."

"She must be weak in the head," said Hubert, "fainting that way and all."

"Quite possibly," said Sir Jarvis as the ghosts faded away. "Too much inbreeding in the royal lines, you know."

"Chartreuse!" said Grassina, shaking her. "Wake up! You can't stay here." When her sister didn't respond, she slapped her once on each cheek.

Chartreuse opened her eyes. "What are you doing? What happened?"

"You fainted. If you stand up, we'll . . ."

"Don't make up stories, Grassina." Chartreuse pushed herself up with her elbows. "I've never fainted in my life. I'm not one of those weak-kneed Nellies who can't . . . What is *that*?"

The fog had moved on, but something else was coming their way. A shape even darker than the deepest shadows was drifting toward them out of the gloom. About the size of a calf, it had glittering red eyes that glared malevolently at them. Chartreuse scrambled to her feet, clutching Grassina's hand for support. "Let's go, Grassina. Let's get out of here."

"I'd love to, except we have to go that way to get to the stairs," Grassina replied, gesturing toward the corridor past the shadow beast.

Grassina could feel her sister's hand tremble as they backed away. She suddenly had the urge to protect her, a feeling so unfamiliar that she surprised herself, but Chartreuse was her last living relative, or at least the last one who felt like family. As Chartreuse took another step back, the red eyes swung in her direction.

"Don't move, Chartreuse," said Grassina, but it was too late. The shadow beast was charging straight at her older sister.

"Oh no, you don't," shouted Grassina. Pulling back her fist, she stepped in front of Chartreuse and punched the shadow squarely between its glowing red eyes. With an anguished howl, the shadow beast stopped in its tracks, turned tail, and ran the other way.

"Thank goodness," said Chartreuse, her voice sounding as unsteady as she looked. Tidying her hair with one hand, she took the torch from Grassina and started for the stairs, going faster when she heard the tap of her own footsteps. Grassina was right behind her when she reached the top. As the dungeon door closed behind them, Grassina started to say good night, but Chartreuse didn't give her the chance.

"Don't you dare say a word. For once I want you to listen to what I have to say. I told you I didn't want to go down there, but you insisted. We had to go see Father, who wasn't even there. And you said that Mother was gone, except she wasn't! And then you stood there like a stick when . . . when something tried to frighten me to death, and then there was that *monster!* Were you trying to get me killed? That was it, wasn't it? You've always been jealous of me. You spoiled my lessons so my magic wouldn't start and laughed at me when I tried to learn in spite of you. You hate me so much that you want to see me dead. I think you want to see all of us dead. I bet you were happy that Father died. I bet those tears were all a pretense. You're just as bad as Mother. You don't even need a curse to turn you into a horrible person. You were born that way. Do us both a favor and stay away from me. I don't ever want to hear you or any of your ideas again. I wish you weren't my sister. I wish you'd never been born!"

Grassina was stunned. She knew that encountering the ghosts and the shadow beast had rattled Chartreuse, but even that wouldn't account for all the horrible things she'd said. Grassina watched, gasping for air as Chartreuse whirled around and strode down the hall.

Eleven

rassina didn't sleep at all that night, although she tried for the first few hours. After that, she wrapped herself in her blanket and curled up on the window ledge to gaze at the night sky. She didn't know what to do. The life she'd always known was over; nothing would ever be the same again now that her father was gone. Chartreuse would probably become queen soon since she wanted it so much and their mother obviously didn't care. Because Chartreuse seemed to blame Grassina for everything bad that had ever happened, Grassina was sure that one of Chartreuse's first acts as queen of Greater Greensward would be to banish her younger sister. And if she didn't banish Grassina, she'd probably see her married off to one of the least desirable suitors. Perhaps it would be the one who hadn't bathed since the day he was born. Then again, if Chartreuse didn't marry her off, she might keep her at the castle as some sort of slave to appease Olivene, making Grassina do all the nasty chores for their mother. As far as Grassina could see, her future at the castle would be awful no matter what Chartreuse decided.

As the first rays of sunlight turned the night sky from black to gray, Grassina collected a change of clothes and all of her throwing stones, wrapping them in a blanket. Loaded down with this bundle, she was the first person to cross the drawbridge that morning.

Grassina went as far as the edge of the practice field before glancing back at the castle one last time. The sight of the mist-shrouded moat, the pennants floating from the tops of the turrets, and the silvery stone of the castle fortifications almost made her want to cry. "No more of that," Grassina muttered to herself, rubbing her eyes with her free hand. She'd cried enough over the last few days to last her a lifetime and was afraid that if she got started again, she might not be able to stop.

Hurrying past the practice field, she tried not to think about the last time she'd seen her father there, talking and laughing with his men. She ducked her head, refusing to look at the tree house. After bringing Marniekins and Hector back to the castle, she'd left them in a special hiding place in the buttery. She knew it was foolish, but she regretted that she hadn't taken the time to say good-bye. It almost felt as if she'd deserted old friends. And then there was Pippa, a new friend who must think she'd been abandoned, too.

"Pippa!" Grassina called as she passed under the ruined tree house. "Pippa, where are you?"

After pausing for a reply and hearing nothing but silence, Grassina shifted her bundle in her arms and continued walking. Pippa may not have stayed around the tree house, but she still might not have gone far. Calling the little snake's name, Grassina followed her usual route to the swamp, looking for Pippa the entire time.

She was still calling to the snake when she reached the last of the trees that grew at the edge of the swamp. Suddenly, something fell off a branch and landed on her shoulder. Grassina shrieked and dropped her bundle, then began slapping at herself with both hands.

"Hey!" Pippa said, squirming under the neckline of Grassina's tunic to avoid being slapped. "What'ss wrong with you?"

"Help! I . . . Oh, it's you. Why did you do that? You nearly frightened me to death!"

"Ssorry," said Pippa, "except it wass your fault. You kept calling me! I wanted to sstay away from you. After all the bad thingss my luck hass done, I thought you'd be better off without me. But you're my only friend, and when you kept shouting my name, I decided that you musst really need me for ssomething. Iss everything all right?"

Grassina took a deep, shuddering breath, ready to tell the little snake about her father's death and her sister's cruel words, but she found she didn't want to talk about it, at least not yet. Instead she let her eyes wander from the blue sky that seemed to go on forever, to the light reflecting off the water half hidden by cattails, to the bees humming around a patch of wildflowers, and she realized that she felt better than she had in days. Her stomach had been in knots from the last time she spoke with her sister, but now that she had reached the swamp, she was finally able to relax.

"It's been awful, but I think it's about to get a lot better," Grassina told the little snake. After all, she had a friend, a place to go, and the beginning of a plan. She didn't expect the Swamp Fairy to be easy to find. If she hadn't shown herself yet, she wasn't likely to just because it was what Grassina wanted. Even so, Grassina knew exactly what to do. She'd make herself a shelter deep in the swamp at the end of one of the more difficult-to-find paths, somewhere safe where nasty relatives would never find her should they ever think to come looking. She would go out during the day and look for the Swamp Fairy, who was bound to want to meet her face-to-face eventually. Grassina wasn't sure what she would do then, but at least she could thank the only person who'd helped her. In the meantime, there would be plenty to eat, at least for the rest of the summer, and she was sure she'd meet the fairy before the weather grew cold.

Although she doubted that anyone would care enough to try to find her, Grassina planned to hide her trail by stepping on rocks and avoiding the softer mud. Taking the less obvious routes, she could go places that only she knew existed.

"I'm going to live in the swamp for a while. Things have gotten worse at the castle and I have to get away," said Grassina.

"It got worsse when I wassn't even there? Maybe my bad luck rubbed off on you!"

Grassina sighed. "I don't think you have bad luck. If anything, I think your luck is good, at least for you. When that monster broke into the witch's cottage and wrecked everything, he set you free, didn't he?"

"Yess, and sstepped on my tail!"

"Which wasn't bad enough to kill you. Think about what would have happened if he'd stepped on your head!"

"That'ss true," said Pippa. "But what about your little housse in the tree?"

"It was ruined, which was lucky for you when you think about it. I hadn't brought you any food; if the tree hadn't broken the cottage roof, you couldn't have gotten out and found something to eat."

"I never thought of it that way!"

"That's what I mean. It's all a matter of how you look at it. So I don't want to hear any more about your bad luck," Grassina said as she set her feet just so, to avoid the sucking mud.

"All right," Pippa said. "But I have sso many other

thingss I want to tell you. Even though I've been frightfully cold, I've learned a lot during the lasst few dayss. Did you know that dollss can live in trunkss and don't need to breathe?"

"Most of them don't talk either," muttered Grassina.

"What did you ssay?"

"Nothing. What else have you learned?"

"That thosse metal birdss couldn't ssay anything but nonssensse. I don't think they have any real thoughtss in their headss. Mice aren't too bright either. They go the ssame placess time after time, which makess them eassy to catch."

"I'm sure it does," said Grassina.

"And the hairy humanss who run on all fourss are much fasster than the oness who aren't hairy and run on two feet."

Grassina stopped walking. "Hairy humans? Do you mean werewolves? Have you seen any around here?"

"A few. They were on their way to your casstle. They came back talking about the guardss and the fori . . . forfif . . . the moat and wallss and sstuff."

Grassina nodded. "You mean the fortifications. They're the things that keep the castle safe. Have you seen any hairy humans today?" she asked, glancing behind her.

"I never ssee them when the ssun iss out. Do you think they could be related to owlss? Owlss come out at night, too."

"I'm sure there's no connection," said Grassina. "Please do me a favor. Tell me if you see any sign of those hairy humans. I'd like to know where they are and what they're doing."

"Ssure," said Pippa, "although I don't know why anyone would want to talk to them."

While the little snake kept watch for the hairy humans, Grassina followed the secret pathways that only she knew, zigzagging where the hidden path required it, jumping across patches of quickmud to another path when the first arrived at a dead end. She thought she smelled smoke, but the wind changed direction, carrying the odor away before she could locate its source. The possibility of dragons in the area made her walk faster, yet it still took her most of the morning to reach the heart of the swamp.

Grassina knew exactly where she would build her cozy little home. An island about a quarter the size of the Great Hall supported a spring and a scattering of wild plum trees. With its own moat of quicksand and open water surrounding it and a thick screen of trees and brush concealing it, the island was almost impossible to find let alone reach unless one knew exactly where to look. Grassina had visited it many times and was familiar with every tree and rock.

To her surprise, when she arrived at the island the little grove of plum trees was occupied. A makeshift lean-to stood between two of the larger trees. Only a short distance away, a pile of kindling and a still-smoldering log marked a fire pit ringed with stones. Draped over the branch of one of the plum trees, a ragged tunic and a pair of breeches dripped water onto the trampled grass, evidence that someone had been washing laundry. Even so, one quick glance around the tiny island showed her that no one was home.

"Now what will I do?" Grassina murmured.

"Iss *that* where you're going to live?" asked Pippa. "It doessn't look very warm."

"That lean-to isn't mine," said Grassina. "I don't know who made it. It wasn't here the last time I came this way."

She considered turning around and going in search of another likely spot, but her feet refused to obey. Her whole plan had been centered on this island, and to find that living there was no longer an option was almost more than she could bear. Shouldering her bundle, Grassina crossed onto the island and began to look around, wondering who had taken over her secret hiding spot.

The campsite held little of a personal nature. An old wooden trencher and a small iron pot rested on the ground beside the fire pit. Inside the lean-to she found a simple pair of leather shoes in good condition and a neatly folded blanket, clean, sweet smelling, and serviceable despite the patches that seemed to hold it together. She didn't think there was anything else to find until she picked up the blanket and saw that it had been concealing a slim wooden chest. With water marks discoloring the wood and deep grooves and scratches in its top and sides, the chest looked like it might have come from a trash heap, but there was something about it that intrigued her.

Pippa flicked her tongue at the chest. "What'ss that? Iss there a doll like Marniekinss inside? Hello there!" she called, sliding down Grassina's arm so that she was closer to the wooden chest. "Can you hear me?"

"Pippa, not so loud! I don't think a doll would fit in there. Just a minute and I'll see if I can open it." Grassina knelt beside the chest and tried to lift the lid. It stayed shut as stubbornly as if it had been made of one piece.

"That'ss not going to work," said Pippa. "Maybe if you bit it, or hit it with a sstick . . ."

"I think I know a better way," said Grassina.

Determined to know what the interloper on her island might be hiding, Grassina inserted a slim, pointed stick in the tiny gap between the lid and the base, and attempted to pry it open. Aside from jamming her thumbnail, nothing happened, however, so she took the chest in both hands and was shaking it when an angry voice behind her said, "What do you think you're doing?"

Startled, Grassina stood, bumping her head on one of the posts that supported the lean-to. The lean-to tottered and swayed. A strong arm reached out and pulled her to safety just before the shelter fell with a crash. While

Grassina staggered and tried not to fall, Pippa slipped under the neckline of her tunic.

"Ow! What are you doing? Oh...my...," said Grassina, glancing from the scowling boy who had saved her to the jumbled branches that had formed the lean-to moments before. "I'm sorry. I didn't mean to . . ."

The boy let go of her arm and stepped back. "To what? Destroy the only shelter I have or snoop around in my personal possessions?"

"Both. Neither. I mean . . ." Grassina bit her lip. "Wait a minute. I'm not the one in the wrong. You shouldn't even be here. Who are you, anyway?"

"That's not the point," said the boy. "Hey, give me that!" Snatching the dilapidated chest from her hand, he inspected it as carefully as if it were his most precious treasure. Grassina decided that, from the way he was dressed, it probably was. The oversized tunic he wore came down past his knees. His feet were bare like an urchin's and his sandy brown hair was long and uneven, as if he'd trimmed it himself. He was taller than Grassina, although not by much, and she might have been afraid if he hadn't had such an open, honest face and warm brown eyes that would have looked friendly if he weren't so angry.

"Why are you here?" asked the boy, looking up from the chest to glare at her. "You weren't supposed to come anywhere near . . ." His voice trailed off as if he'd said something wrong, leaving Grassina wondering what it might have been. "I mean, no one was supposed to come here. This is my home, and I want to be alone."

"You can't make me leave! I have more right to be here than you do. I'm . . ." It occurred to Grassina that it might not be a good idea to tell this stranger exactly who she was. Although some people might respect her royal status, others might try to use it to their advantage. He didn't look like a bad person, but looks could be deceiving, as her old nurse used to say. Grassina didn't know anything about this boy—who he was, where he came from, and certainly not what his intentions might be should he hear the truth about her.

"You're what?" asked the boy.

"Not leaving, that's all. I spend more time in this swamp than anybody else. What makes you think you can show up all of a sudden and lay claim to it?"

"I'm not claiming the whole swamp, just this island. And I didn't just show up. I've been here for a while."

"Then how come I haven't seen you before?"

The boy shrugged. "I guess you haven't gone to the right places. It doesn't matter though. I built my home here, so this island is mine. You can just—"

"If that's all it takes to claim it, I'm going to build my cottage here, too. It will be a lot better than that thing you had. Your *home* was all crooked and wobbly . . ."

"It was a perfectly good lean-to!" said the boy, sounding indignant.

"It was more of a lean-from, if you ask me!" said Grassina. "I hardly bumped the thing and it fell over."

"Ha!" said the boy. "I doubt you could build anything, let alone a cottage."

"We'll see about that!" said Grassina.

"Fine!" said the boy. "Tell me when you're finished. I could use a good laugh!"

Grassina turned her back on the boy so fast that the end of her braid whipped around and stung her cheek. She was careful not to look his way as she studied the ground, trying to decide where to build her cottage. Finding a level spot, she cleared away the debris and left the island in search of long, straight branches.

Although she'd envisioned the cottage as roomy and large enough to walk around in, she began to think that might not be practical if she was going to build it all by herself. Without an ax or saw, she'd have to take whatever windfall she could find, which wouldn't leave her much to work with. She found a few branches that might suffice, although they weren't nearly as long as she'd hoped.

Grassina was about to start back to the island when Pippa said, "I'll sstay here for a while. I don't want that boy to ssee me."

"I wouldn't let him hurt you, if that's what you're worried about," said Grassina.

"It'ss not that. I don't like meeting new people. You're nicer than mosst sstrangerss. The old witch wouldn't

145

come near me without a forked sstick in her hand. She alwayss looked like she wass afraid I might bite her."

"Would you?"

"Only if I had to, but that'ss besside the point. I think it'ss better if I keep to mysself while you're around him."

Grassina shrugged. "If that's what you want."

"What I want is a nice fat mousse," said Pippa. "But that'ss ssomething elsse I'll have to do on my own."

❧

Thinking about building a shelter was a lot easier than actually building one. It took Grassina a number of botched attempts before she finally found a method that would work. After carefully placing the branches where she wanted them, she lashed them together with willow wands, propping them up again each time they fell down. It was frustrating work, made all the worse because she knew the boy would be watching. When she had the branches angled well enough that they could stand on their own, she covered them with twigs and stuffed the spaces with mud and grass.

Pippa returned shortly before the shelter was finished. "It lookss like an upsside-down bird'ss nesst."

Grassina shrugged. "Maybe, but I'm too tired to care."

"What'ss that noisse?" asked Pippa.

Rubbing her growling stomach, Grassina said, "I'm hungry, that's all. I haven't eaten all day." She glanced at the boy, wondering if he was watching her, but he was still reinforcing the lean-to he'd rebuilt and didn't seem to notice her.

"Sso, are you going to call that boy over to ssee what you did?" asked Pippa. "I'll wait in the grasss if you are. You sure showed him, making thiss housse and all. It'ss sso much better than that thing he built."

"Not really," said Grassina. "It isn't at all what I wanted to make. It's not a cottage. It isn't even big enough to call a hovel."

"That'ss all right. You don't have to show him anything. We don't want to look like we're bragging."

The sun was setting, and with the advent of nightfall came a cool breeze and the scent of rain. Grassina shivered and slipped into her cottage on her hands and knees, avoiding the still-wet mud in the walls. She was cold, her skin felt grimy, and her stomach ached with hunger. It was hard not to think about all that she'd given up—hot food, a roof over her head, clean, dry clothes, and the safety of solid stone walls. While Grassina pried a small rock out of the ground so it wouldn't dig into her side when she lay down, Pippa investigated the little bit of floor space, then slithered up the wall and disappeared among the branches.

Grassina's tiny cottage creaked as the wind picked up, finding its way through the holes she'd missed. Wrapping herself in her blanket, she huddled in the center of her shelter, yawning so hard she could hear her jaw creak. A larger gust shook her shelter, and Pippa dropped out of the ceiling. Gathering the little snake to her, Grassina curled around her friend, trying to warm her. When the wind died down for a minute, she thought she heard the boy talking, but then the rain began and the gentle tapping lulled Grassina into an exhausted sleep. Even after the rain became a steady downpour, she did little more than pull her blanket over her head and continue sleeping. As the rain grew heavier, globs of mud washed through the chinks in the walls and ceiling. *Plip! Plip!* Cold mud dripped on her blanket, trickling down her hunched figure and turning the blanket into a sodden weight.

"You might want to get out of there before this thing collapses," the boy said from the doorway, but Grassina was sleeping too deeply to hear him.

She didn't wake when Pippa slipped away, or when the boy sighed and crept into her shelter on his hands and knees, then carried her out, still wrapped in the saturated blanket. As the rain lashed them both, the boy held Grassina closer, smiling to himself when she snuggled into the warmth of his arms.

It wasn't until Grassina smelled meat roasting over an open fire that she finally opened her eyes. The sun had risen, making the drops quivering on the leaves of the closest plum tree shimmer like diamonds in a world washed clean by the night's rain. A small flock of sparrows flitted among the branches, greeting the day and each other with a chirping chorus. Confused when she didn't see the stone walls of her chamber, Grassina threw off the dry blanket that covered her and sat up. Even as the events of the previous day came back to her, she couldn't remember leaving the shelter she had built.

The smell of roasting meat was too hard to resist. Grassina climbed out from under the boy's lean-to, rubbing her back to ease the stiffness. The boy must have helped her; it was his blanket that had been covering her when she awoke, and she couldn't imagine how else she could have ended up in the lean-to. Before approaching the fire pit and the source of the tempting smells, she glanced around the clearing, expecting to see the boy. She saw her shoes, clean and drying in the sun, as well as her own soggy blanket draped over a branch, but the boy was nowhere to be found. Pippa was gone as well.

Peeking inside the shelter she had built, Grassina was dismayed at how poorly it had survived the rain. She thought the sagging roof was bad enough until she saw the mud puddle where she had sat the night before. Shuddering, she backed away and hurried to the fire pit.

Some sort of small animal had been skinned, skewered, and left with the stick resting across two forked twigs. The scent of fat sizzling on the coals of the fire was almost more than she could bear, but she rotated the stick to cook it on the other side, still expecting the boy at any moment. When he wasn't back by the time the meat began to char, she took it off the fire and blew on its golden brown surface to hasten its cooling. With no sign of the boy, Grassina could wait no longer. She tore into the crisped morsels, savoring the flavor while watching the pathway for the boy's return. Although she intended to eat only half, she was licking her fingers before she knew it, having already cleaned the bones.

After one last disgusted glance at the sorry shelter she'd made, Grassina decided that it was time to begin searching for the Swamp Fairy. While she was at it, she'd see if she could find the boy. She would thank him, but she'd also let him know that she didn't really need assistance and could take care of herself.

Grassina spent the rest of the day visiting many of the places she'd frequented before her mother had changed. She went deep into the swamp where only muskrats, otters, and wildfowl left their prints. She circled the quagmire, collecting useful herbs that grew at its edge and nibbling berries as she picked them. At the pond that bordered the enchanted forest, Grassina kept an eye open for werewolf prints like the ones she'd seen before and was relieved when she failed to find any. She did smell smoke, however, and followed it to a patch of weeds that had been crisped in a fire. Because the burn mark was so small that only a very young dragon could have made it, she decided that it wasn't worth worrying about.

The shadows were lengthening when Grassina returned

to the island with a sack full of edible roots and found that the boy was there ahead of her. He offered her some plums and a seat beside the fire where two leaf-wrapped fish baked amid the coals.

"Where did you go?" Grassina asked, watching the boy poke the steaming fish with a stick.

"Someone had to catch our dinner," the boy replied without looking up.

Grassina opened her sack to offer him some of the edible roots. "You didn't have to get one for me. I can fend for myself when I have to."

"I'm sure you can," he replied, looking pointedly at her sagging shelter.

"Who are you anyway?" Grassina asked. "How did you end up here?"

"My name is Haywood. I ran away from home. I couldn't live there anymore, not the way things were with my father. So I came here looking for someplace where I could be by myself."

"Then I guess you couldn't have found a better place than the swamp," said Grassina. "No one comes here except me . . . and the Swamp Fairy, of course."

Haywood chuckled. "The Swamp Fairy! That's a good one."

"Shh! Don't laugh. She might hear you. You don't want to make her angry."

Haywood gave her an incredulous look. "You don't

really believe . . . I guess you do," he said, seeing how serious Grassina looked.

"Of course I believe in the Swamp Fairy. She's helped me more than once. Why, if it weren't for her, I'd be a snail or something even worse."

"Really?" said Haywood. "And what exactly did this Swamp Fairy do?"

"She sent a toad when I needed one and later a flock of blackbirds with eggshells."

"How thoughtful of her. But if she's so busy helping people, I wonder why I've never seen her."

"I think she must be shy," said Grassina. "To tell the truth, I haven't seen her either."

"Here," said Haywood. "I think these are ready." Using one of the longer sticks, he deftly flipped the leaf-wrapped fish out of the fire and onto a flat rock to cool.

"You're a good cook," Grassina told him between bites a few minutes later.

"Thanks," he said. "You'd be surprised at all the things I can do."

Twelve

Although Grassina hoped to get up before Haywood left the next morning, he was already gone when the touch of the sun's rays on her eyelids woke her. Grassina had meant to repair her shelter and sleep there, but nightfall had taken her by surprise, and she hadn't done more than clean out some of the mud before it was too dark to see. The boy had let her sleep under his lean-to again while he slept at the opposite end. Grassina appreciated that, after that one meaningful glance, he never again referred to the deplorable condition of the shelter she'd built. Even so, she was well aware of how few things she'd actually accomplished since she'd arrived in the swamp and how bleak her future looked. It was almost enough to make her want to pull the blanket over her head and never come out from under it.

"Are you going to eat thiss egg or what?" asked Pippa. The little snake was curled beside an egg that had been carefully placed just beyond the lean-to. "That boy boiled it in hiss pot and left it for you. I prefer them raw, but I'm willing to give it a try if you don't want it. We could call it my good luck and—"

"I'll eat it," Grassina said, reaching for the egg. "Who knows when I'll get something else? Finding food has been harder than I thought it would be. And don't you dare tell me it's because I have bad luck. Sometimes luck has nothing to do with what happens."

"Hmm," said Pippa. "Sso tell me, why do you ssup-posse the boy takess that box with him when he leavess? Maybe it'ss a deep, dark ssecret. Maybe he keepss the fin-ger boness of a murderer in it. Or maybe there are love notess from a jilted mermaid, or a horde of deadly sspi-derss trained to jump up and bite you on the nosse when you leasst expect it."

"That's a horrible thought," said Grassina. "Where do you get such ideas?"

Pippa coiled herself on Grassina's knee and rested her head on her tail. "I didn't make them up. They were part of a sspell Mudine ussed once."

"So why do you suppose Haywood takes the box with him?" asked Grassina.

"Either he takess it becausse he needss ssomething that'ss in it, or sso ssomeone, maybe you, can't ssee what'ss insside."

"I wonder which it was."

"My guesss iss," said Pippa, "it'ss probably both. Ssay,

154

are you going to eat the resst of that egg? Becausse if you're not . . ."

"I'm eating it! See!" Grassina took her second bite.

Pippa eyed a bird's nest at the top of a plum tree. "Then I ssupposse I have to go get my own food. I feel a ssudden yearning for fresh eggss, sso if you'll excusse me . . ."

Grassina finished the egg while following the path off the island. It had occurred to her that the fairy might have left the swamp on some sort of errand, but she wasn't ready to give up yet. However, she was beginning to wonder just what she would say if she found the fairy. Should she ask for a place to live? A new family, perhaps? But even that wouldn't work. The only family she really wanted was the one she'd had. Then a thought occurred to her that was so stupendous that she gasped and almost forgot to start breathing again. Maybe she could ask the fairy to use her magic to remove the curse from the queen and put everything back the way it had been. Then her father would be alive and Chartreuse wouldn't hate her and . . . How strong was fairy magic anyway?

Having started the day feeling dispirited, Grassina now had a spring in her step and a new purpose to her search. Finding the fairy could change not only her life, but that of her entire family. All she knew about the family curse was what her father had told her, so maybe it wouldn't be too hard to end.

"Swamp Fairy!" called Grassina as she waded through the tall grass beside the bottomless pit. "Oh, Swamp Fairy," she shouted across the river where the otters made their home. "Are you there, Swamp Fairy?" she wailed.

Although she searched high and low for the Swamp Fairy, Grassina never saw any evidence that the fairy was around. She was on her way back when she passed another patch of weeds burned to a crunchy black, a patch that had been lush and green the day before. Grassina shrugged and continued on, once again certain that she had nothing to fear. It was probably just a baby dragon, although she had yet to see or hear one.

It was late in the day when Grassina returned to the island and found Haywood there with dinner waiting. This time he'd found enough meat and edible roots to make a stew. Grassina had found a handful of scraggly wild onions.

"How did you find all this food?" she asked as she accepted a hollowed-out gourd filled with stew.

"Magic!" Haywood said with a wink.

Grassina shrugged. "So don't tell me." She wasn't about to pester him into telling her, not when she already planned to find out for herself. "But I have another question for you. I've been finding burned spots like a baby dragon might make. And I found werewolf prints near the enchanted forest, but that was before I came here to live. Have you seen any sign of either one?"

Haywood bent over the pot on the fire, stirring the little bit of stew that remained. "Can't say that I have," he said without looking up.

"Good," said Grassina. "Just let me know if you do."

Once again, Grassina was too tired to work on her shelter, but this time, she had another reason to go to bed early. While Haywood was banking the fire for the night, she found Pippa soaking up the last bit of heat from a sun-warmed rock on the other side of the island. "Would you wake me before Haywood leaves tomorrow morning?" she asked the snake. "You could get me up when you get up."

"If you really want me to," said Pippa.

"I do," Grassina said. "But we have to be quiet about it. I want to follow him without him knowing it."

"I get it. You want to sspy on him. And you should, too. I bet there'ss something he issn't telling you that you really should know." The little snake reared her head. "Maybe your mother ssent him to sspy on *you*!"

"He was here before I was, remember? He couldn't have been sent to spy on me before I even decided to come here."

"Well, there iss that . . . ," said the snake.

"Did you say something?" Haywood asked, coming up behind her.

Pippa slithered off into the tall grass as Grassina turned to face him. "No, I was just talking to myself."

"You do that a lot."

"I do not!"

"Yes, you do. I've seen you when you didn't know I was looking. You do it all the time."

"You do spy on me!"

Haywood blushed and looked away. "I wouldn't call it spying. I just like to look at you. I think you're beautiful."

Grassina felt heat creep up her neck and across her cheeks. "People usually call my sister beautiful, not me. Please don't say things you don't mean."

"I don't," Haywood said, shaking his head vehemently. "I think you're the most beautiful girl I've ever seen."

"Then I thank you for the compliment," Grassina said, feeling her cheeks flame. Although her father had often told her that she was pretty, no one else ever had. She had always assumed that her father had said it *because* he was her father.

A bat darted between them, catching an insect, then zigzagging away. "It's getting dark," Haywood said into the uncomfortable silence.

Grassina nodded and turned toward the lean-to. She was suddenly aware of him in a way she hadn't been before. The feeling stayed with her as she wrapped herself in her own now-dry blanket under the lean-to and closed her eyes. Hayward was good-looking in a sweet and wholesome way. His tousled brown hair was getting lighter from the sun and was now the color of drying hay.

His eyes, so angry at first, were friendly, and the crinkles in the corners made him seem that much nicer. She had believed him when he'd said he was telling the truth simply because she didn't think he was capable of lying. Tired as she was, it took her a long time to fall asleep that night.

It was still dark out when Grassina felt something brush her cheek. The feather-light touch came again, and she opened her eyes. In the radiance of the nearly full moon she could just make out Pippa's slight form only inches away, flicking her tongue at her. Startled, Grassina jerked her head back, thumping it on one of the support posts.

"You ssaid you wanted me to wake you," said the snake.

Grassina cleared her throat, careful to be quiet so she wouldn't wake Haywood. "Thanks," she said. "What time is it anyway?"

"I'm a ssnake. Do you really think I can tell time? That lasst mole I ate didn't agree with me. I've had indigesstion ever ssince I sswallowed it. I think it musst have gone bad. Well-behaved moless never give me problemss like thiss."

Grassina glanced up at the moon to check its position in the sky. "Will you look at that! It can't be later than five o'clock. I wonder why Haywood gets up so early."

"He doessn't. I did becausse my sstomach hurtss. Can I help it if I couldn't ssleep any longer? You ssaid you

159

wanted me to wake you when I got up. That boy will probably ssleep for a while yet."

"What am I supposed to do in the meantime?"

"Go back to ssleep?"

"Will you wake me again?"

"Why, wassn't once enough for you?"

"But I . . . But you . . ."

"Now that I'm awake, I have thingss to do. Nestss to raid. Mice to catch. Maybe a nice tender mousseling will make my sstomach feel better."

"If I go back to sleep, I'll probably miss him again."

"You probably will, the way your luck iss going now. I guesss you should sstay awake," said the snake, and she disappeared into the underbrush.

Squirming around so that she was almost sitting, Grassina propped herself on her elbows. She couldn't sit up all the way because it wouldn't do for Haywood to wake and see that she was awake as well, not if she wanted to keep it a secret.

Something plopped into the water just beyond the last plum tree. A tiny creature squeaked in the grasp of a night predator. Grassina pulled the blanket up to her chin and watched the stars through the shifting branches overhead. She thought about the tapestry that had hung on the wall of her mother's chamber for as long as she could remember. The tapestry had shown her mother as a young woman standing on one of the castle's towers. It was night, and the stars were actually twinkling, just like the ones in the sky were now. Her mother had called it the Green Witch Tapestry and said that she had received it when she became the Green Witch. She never would tell Grassina any details, just that it had appeared in her room the night her own mother had died. The tapestry had disappeared when the curse changed Olivene, and no one had seen it since.

Grassina was still thinking about the tapestry when she heard Haywood begin to stir. She remained motionless while he crawled out from under the lean-to and made soft noises by the fire pit. When she finally opened her eyes, he wasn't on the path she always took; he was going in the opposite direction on a path she hadn't known existed and had the wooden chest tucked under his arm.

Watching from among the plum trees, Grassina saw him follow a convoluted set of twists and turns. She couldn't understand how he knew where to place his feet with such apparent confidence until she reached the head of the path. Two parallel rows of fireflies sat facing each other across a span of a foot or so on what she would have sworn was quicksand, lighting the way in an on-again, off-again pattern. If she hadn't seen Haywood place his feet exactly *there*, she never would have thought it safe enough to try. Grassina's steps were tentative at first, but when she found firm ground beneath the top layer of mud and water, she began to walk with more confidence.

The sun rose, banishing the fireflies and replacing them with thick-bodied black beetles, lined up like dots of ink splattered across one of her father's parchments. When the water-laden sand thickened around her like curdled milk, supporting straggly plants and not much else on its more solid-looking clumps, bright yellow butterflies fanned their wings on the only tufts that could hold her weight.

Grassina glanced up to see Haywood step onto dry land and hurry around a group of blue green leaved shrubs. She took the last few steps faster than was prudent, and her foot slipped into the water, making her half fall, half jump to solid ground. Bunching the fabric of her skirt in her fists, she ran after Haywood, convinced that she knew his secret.

It took her a few minutes to find him again as tall grass concealed where he knelt beside one of the larger ponds. A fat, silver-sided fish lay gasping at his feet, and another leaped out of the water as she watched.

"So that's it," she said, pointing an accusing finger at him. "You can do magic!"

Haywood turned to look at her, his face a study of flickering emotions. "How did you get here?" he asked. "I thought you were asleep."

"I wanted to see where you went," Grassina said. "I never guessed . . ."

"So now you know," he said, his voice sounding stiff

162

and wooden. "I suppose this means I'll never see you again."

"Why do you say that?"

Haywood shrugged. "If you're like any of the girls I used to know, you'll be afraid of me. If you're like my father, you'll threaten to have me locked up for the rest of my 'miserable' life."

Grassina was horrified. "Is that why you ran away? And they acted like that just because you can do magic? I can't see how anyone who knew you would ever think that you would hurt anyone, and to say that you—"

An incredulous look crept across Haywood's face. "You mean you aren't afraid of me? I thought you of all people would . . . I mean, with a mother like yours . . ."

"You know who my mother is?"

"I know she's a witch who threatened to turn you into things if you didn't do what she wanted. That's enough to make anyone afraid of magic."

"How do you know she did that? I never mentioned anything about it."

"I told you, I've heard you talking to yourself. I've been living in the swamp for a few weeks now. The first time I saw you, you were holding a toad. I heard you say that you needed a toad with seven warts for your mother. And then you came looking for blackbird eggshells. Both times you talked about what your mother would do if you didn't bring her what she wanted."

Grassina's hand flew to her heart. "It was you, wasn't it? You're the one who helped me, not the Swamp Fairy! I saw what you could do with insects and fish. I suppose toads and birds wouldn't be very different."

Haywood shrugged and shifted the wooden box to his other arm. "I can do only simple magic—the most basic kind that even the least gifted fey can do, like turn flax into gold and make ants separate peas from lentils. I've tried to do more involved spells, but I can get them to work only partway before they fizzle out. So far, I haven't been able to control any animal bigger than a cat."

"At least you can do some kind of magic!" said Grassina. "Even small magic is better than nothing."

"Small magic, huh? I suppose that's an appropriate name for it. I haven't given up on doing the bigger magic, though. I was trying to come up with a bigger, better spell when my sister and her friend walked in on me. I lost my concentration, and there was an accident that set the stable on fire. They couldn't wait to tell my father their version of what had happened. He never gave me a chance to explain."

"But I thought people respected magic users. The Green Witch . . ."

". . . is well respected. I know. And, because of her, so are most of the women who do magic. But men are different. How often do you hear about a good wizard? They're out there, but it's very rare to hear about the good they've

164

done. People would rather talk about the ones who misuse their magic, which makes it seem as if they all do."

"You're a good person. Surely your father could see . . ."

"My father didn't know me well enough to *see* anything. I was the fifth of seven brothers and three sisters and had never been his favorite, probably because I didn't fit into his plans. Unlike my brothers, I didn't want to be a knight or a member of the clergy. I practiced with the sword and lance when Father demanded it, but everyone knew I preferred my books. My mother had given me an illustrated bestiary shortly before she died birthing my youngest sister. The book showed every magical creature known to man. I thought they were fascinating and spent all my spare time learning everything I could about magical beasts. When my father found out, he took my books away and ordered me to practice swordplay with my brothers. I disarmed the two eldest, which seemed to anger the rest. Father didn't say a word when they all took me on at once, fresh and eager to fight while I was too tired to hold up my sword."

"That's awful!" said Grassina.

Haywood shrugged. "It wasn't that unusual in our family. My father often turned a blind eye when it suited him. Last year, I discovered that I had some small talent for magic, so I went off by myself whenever I could, hoping that I'd become good enough to make him proud of me. But it was already easy for him to think the worst of me, so he believed my sister when she accused me of purposely setting the stable on fire. You have known me only a short time, yet you've seen me more clearly than he ever did."

"Weren't you able to save any of your books? Oh!" said Grassina. "Is that what you keep inside that wooden box? You take it with you everywhere you go, but I've never seen you open it. Is it the book your mother gave you? If it is, I'd love to see it. I think that book sounds fascinating."

Haywood glanced down at the box. "It's not a book. It's something else. . . . Something too dangerous to open when anyone else is around. I keep it with me in case of an emergency and so no one will try to open it and get hurt. Now I have a question for you. I know you have a pet snake. Don't deny it," he said when Grassina opened her mouth to speak. "It's left trails all over the island. And I've seen you wearing it on your wrist like a bracelet. Why do you keep a snake like that? You're the first girl I've ever met who actually likes snakes."

"I don't like all snakes, just Pippa," said Grassina. "I met her after my mother turned me into a rabbit. Pippa's not a pet, either. She's more of a friend. I'd introduce you to her now, but she's hunting back on the island."

"Good," said Haywood. "There were too many mice there before you came. They were nibbling holes in everything, and I couldn't keep food from one day to the next."

"Thank you," said Grassina.

"For what? I should be the one thanking you. You brought the snake."

Grassina shook her head. "Thank you for helping me when no one else would. I hate to think what I'd be doing now if I'd stayed with my mother and sister."

"In that case, you're welcome," said Haywood. "Although to tell the truth, having you here has been the best thing that ever happened to me."

Thirteen

$\mathcal{L}$ ater that night, Grassina sought out Pippa and suggested that the little snake meet Haywood. "No," said Pippa. "I heard you talking about hiss magic. If he'ss a wizard, he might put me in a cage like Mudine'ss."

"But I won't let him," said Grassina as she carried the little snake toward the campfire where Haywood waited.

"Make him promisse that he won't," said Pippa. "Tell him how horrible it iss to be locked insside a little box. It makess an animal go crazy."

"All right," said Grassina. "I'll make sure he understands."

Haywood was watching her approach with a quizzical expression on his face. "Who are you talking to?" he asked.

Grassina sighed. She wouldn't have to be a translator if only he could talk to animals, too. Hiding her hand behind her back, she stepped closer to the light of the fire. "I was talking to Pippa. She doesn't want to meet you unless you promise never to lock her in a cage."

Haywood smiled and shrugged. "Tell her I promise."

"She wants me to tell you how horrible it is."

"I'm sure she's right," he said, his smile becoming a little less bright.

"So will you promise?" she asked.

"I promise," said Haywood, although he seemed distracted.

"In that case," Grassina said, bringing her hand from behind her back, "this is Pippa!"

The little snake eyed him warily while Grassina told her about Haywood's promise. Turning her head, Pippa whispered to Grassina, who listened, then laughed out loud. "She says she's going to keep her eyes on you. She thought you were nice enough as a regular human, but she isn't so sure now that she knows you're a wizard. She says you have to be nice to me or you'll have to answer to her."

"I'll keep that in mind," Haywood said, looking as serious as he sounded.

Over the next few days, Haywood and Grassina fell into a routine of chores and practice sessions in which he tried to strengthen and expand his collection of spells. Grassina told him about some of the spells that she remembered from watching Chartreuse's lessons and was delighted when Haywood was able to work many of them.

One day, Haywood used his own kind of magic to

make a school of fish gather water grasses and weave them into a basket for Grassina. She was delighted and promptly used it to collect wild mushrooms and roots to add to their supper. When she returned from her excursion, the sky was overcast and there was a chill to the air, so she settled down to watch while Haywood tried to fashion a witches' ball. His first few attempts to make the hovering balls of light fizzled before they'd even left his hands, but eventually he was able to produce one with a faint, wavering glow that could float on its own. Grassina was admiring it when the first fat raindrops splatted on the plum trees.

Although Haywood and Grassina hurried to the shelter of the lean-to, the storm hit so quickly that they were both drenched before they could get inside. Within minutes, the wind was whipping the branches of the plum trees in a creaking frenzy and shearing the top off the water surrounding the island so that it mixed with the driving rain, soaking them until there wasn't a dry scrap of clothing between them. Grassina shivered, her teeth chattering so hard that her jaw hurt. As the wind buffeted the lean-to until it swayed and shook, Haywood drew Grassina to his side and wrapped his blanket around them both.

Lightning split the sky over the enchanted forest. A few seconds later, thunder rumbled like an angry dragon. "Tell me about yourself," Haywood said, slipping his arm around her shoulders.

"Now?" Grassina asked.

"I can't think of a better time," he said. "Why don't I start. I like to read and—"

Thunder occasionally drowned out his words, yet Haywood kept talking. He told her about his childhood, his sisters and their quests for husbands, his brothers and what they expected to inherit from their father. He didn't tell any extraordinary stories, yet Grassina found them interesting because they were about him. They also provided a distraction from the ferocity of the storm around them, which she decided was what he probably had in mind.

For a full two minutes, lightning struck so close that the air smelled acrid and their ears rang from the boom of the thunder. Haywood put both of his arms around her then, and she snuggled into his shoulder, hiding her face until the lightning moved on. She was frightened, but not too frightened to notice that he kissed the top of her head and held her closer.

Because the dark of the storm blended into the dark of night, they had no idea what time the storm ended or when they finally fell asleep. Waking early the next morning, they found that a large portion of the lean-to had collapsed and that the rest was badly in need of repair. The little hut that Grassina had built was completely destroyed, ending the pretense that she was ever going to fix it.

"Well," said Haywood as he surveyed the damage to the

lean-to. "I guess it's time to make a real shelter, something that will stand up under any weather."

Retrieving the cooking pot from a bed of mud, Grassina poured out the water that filled it. "How are you going to do that?" she asked.

"I'll use magic!" he said. "I don't know why I didn't think of it before."

Grassina was hanging things up to dry when a flood of muskrats arrived, dragging saplings and a few larger branches. When the muskrats left, the birds came, bringing so many reeds and twigs that soon there wasn't enough room to stand. After a score of robins nearly dropped their deliveries on her, Grassina picked up her basket and left the island. Rather than trying to watch from a distance, she decided that she wanted to do something nice for Haywood. It didn't take much to persuade Pippa to go with her once the little snake realized that Haywood's hammering was frightening away her usual prey.

Recalling some berry bushes that grew beside the lake fronting the enchanted forest, Grassina picked her way across the uneven ground, avoiding sinkholes and mud pits. The bushes were easy to find, the berries more plentiful than she remembered.

She was unwrapping the little snake from around her wrist when Pippa said, "I don't know why I had to come with you. It'ss not like I can help you pick berriess."

"I told you," said Grassina. "I need you to keep watch

172

for me. This is where I saw those paw prints. Just look around and tell me if you see anything unusual."

"I'd rather take a nap," grumbled the little snake. "My sstomach iss sso full I can hardly move. I should never have eaten a rat that wass too fat to run."

"You slept all the way here," said Grassina, setting Pippa on the ground.

"And it wassn't nearly enough," said the snake.

While Pippa slithered off to explore, Grassina began plucking the riper berries, popping a few in her mouth now and then as she moved from one bush to the next. Her basket was close to overflowing when she thought to look for the little snake again, but Pippa was nowhere to be found.

"Pippa!" Grassina said, inspecting the ground under the bushes. "Pippa!" she called, searching the bank on the swamp side of the lake.

Unable to find her, she paused for a moment as she tried to decide what to do and was surprised to hear Pippa's voice carrying across the water. "She'ss not like mosst humanss. Grasssina is actually nice," said the snake.

Although she really didn't want to go anywhere near the enchanted forest, Grassina had no choice if she wanted to collect her friend. Arming herself with two smooth stones, she rounded the pond and stepped from bright sunlight into the deep shade of the forest. She followed Pippa's voice beneath the ancient trees, certain the whole time that all sorts of creatures were watching her.

When she finally spotted the little snake at the base of a towering oak, Pippa appeared to be talking to a young woman dressed all in white. With her pale skin and mass of auburn hair, the woman almost didn't look real. Grassina took another step and nearly stumbled over a tree root. She glanced down to get her balance; when she looked up again, the little snake was alone.

"Psst! Pippa!" said Grassina. "What are you doing here? It's time to—"

Twigs snapped in the forest. Seconds later, a doe hurtled over a rotting tree stump and darted toward Grassina. Veering to avoid her, it panted, "Hurry! It's coming!"

Pippa swung her head around to face Grassina. "It'ss bad luck that you came now," said the snake. "Lissten to me and don't assk questionss. Climb that tree and don't sstop until you can't go any higher. There iss a beasst on itss way that you don't want to meet."

Grassina stared at her, too astonished to move. "Go!" Pippa said as a pulsating rumble reached Grassina's ears. Shoving the stones back into her sack, Grassina turned to the gnarled old tree behind her and strained to pull herself onto the lowest branch. Her feet scrabbled against the rough bark, and then she was up, clutching the branch until she could get her legs under her.

The sound grew louder, becoming the *whump, whump* of mighty wings. Three deer darted under the tree Grassina was climbing. She needed no encouragement to grab the next branch and the next after that. A buck bounded into sight when she was halfway up the tree. Then a shape as dark as night and the size of three of her father's biggest horses smashed through the forest, shattering branches as it descended on the unfortunate deer. It was a dragon, dark on dark in the gloom of the forest, its eyes and claws appearing to glitter with a light of their own. The buck leaped again, but the dragon met it in midair, snapping its neck with one bite.

Grassina wrapped both arms around a sturdy branch and squeezed her eyes shut, her breath coming in high-pitched wheezes as she tried not to scream. "That'ss a big one," whispered Pippa from beside Grassina's ear. "It musst be a male. The maless sseem to be bigger than the femaless. I came to the foresst after the tree broke your little housse. I've sseen dragonss of all ssizes here."

Grassina bit her lip and tried not to listen to the crunching of bones and tearing of flesh. She didn't dare open her mouth for fear of the sounds that might come out.

"They tear their food apart like that before they sstart eating. You know, I've been thinking. My luck iss pretty good. Here I am in the foresst with monssterss all around, but I'm too ssmall for any of them to care about, whereass you're probably jusst what they'd like. If anybody hass bad luck, I think it'ss you. Look, he'ss almosst finished. He'll be leaving ssoon."

The forest was growing darker when the beast finally

abandoned the remains of the deer carcass and flew off, the beat of its wings creating miniature tornadoes that swirled leaves and broken bits of branches in its wake. Grassina fought to stay in the tree, tightening her already fierce grip on the branch. Because her quaking muscles had been locked in one position for so long, she was in no condition to climb down even after the forest grew quiet. Instead, she struggled to reach one of the wider branches where she could sit for a moment. Her arms and legs were still shaking when she leaned back against the trunk, took deep breaths to calm herself, and willed her heart rate to return to normal.

Grassina was resting on the branch when she heard a sound at the base of the tree. Leaning forward, she glanced down, freezing as a silver body passed below her. It was a wolf, its coat shining in the darkening gloom. As she watched, the wolf raised its head and looked directly at her. For an instant, Grassina could have sworn their eyes met, but it turned away and went on, sniffing the air as it walked.

The wolf paused and raised its head. Grassina shrank back against the tree as the beast's hackles rose, its lips contracted in a fearsome sneer, and a low growl rumbled from its throat. Although she was far enough above the ground that the wolf couldn't possibly reach her, Grassina pulled herself onto a higher branch before looking down again. The wolf had turned so it was facing away from the tree, back the way it had come. Even from behind, the wolf's flattened ears showed its dislike for whatever was approaching.

Grassina looked past the wolf to the darkness beneath the trees and gasped when she saw a figure there, keeping to the thickest shadows, its belly so low it nearly brushed the ground. Another appeared behind it and another after that until half a dozen indistinct shapes surrounded the wolf. When one passed through a patch of moonlight, Grassina caught her first real glimpse of it and had to press the back of her hand against her mouth so as not to cry out. It was a wolf, yet not a wolf, its body chunkier, its head coarser, its paws broader. Grassina shuddered: it was a werewolf.

Although she wanted to look away, Grassina found herself unable to stop watching as the largest one detached itself from the shadows and walked stiff-legged toward the real wolf. "The girl is mine," the werewolf growled.

"Then come and take her," snarled the silver wolf, stepping away.

As the werewolf advanced, the silver wolf waited until they were only a few yards apart before it lunged, landing on the werewolf's back, sending them both tumbling across the ground. Snarling, they raked each other with their claws, ripping at ears and faces, throats and backs in a tangled frenzy of fangs. When they separated, blood flowed freely from gashes on the silver wolf's neck and shoulders as it stood panting, head hanging, feet splayed.

The werewolf was not even winded; the bleeding from its face and throat was not enough to slow the beast as it paced a circle around the silver wolf.

Although she didn't know the silver wolf, Grassina knew that she didn't want the werewolf to win. Opening her sack, she took out a fistful of stones, braced her body with her feet and legs, then hurled the stones one at a time at the werewolf with all the strength she could muster. The first stone hit a glancing blow, making the werewolf snap at its side as if at a biting fly. The second stone hit the werewolf behind the ear. The beast turned its head and was struck on the snout, which made it yelp with pain. Another stone hit it directly between the eyes with such force that its head snapped back and blood oozed in a line across its brow. The werewolf staggered and fell to the ground. When their leader didn't get up, the rest of the pack stepped out of the shadows, the fur along their spines bristling. As they drew closer, Grassina could hear their deep-throated growling all the way up in her tree.

Forming a circle around the silver wolf, the werewolves had begun to move in when the lead werewolf groaned and lurched to its feet. It looked groggy and uncoordinated as it shambled unsteadily back the way it had come. The other werewolves stayed in their circle until a sharp bark from their leader made them turn and slink away into the darkness.

Once the werewolves were gone, the silver wolf

heaved a loud sigh, then collapsed in slow motion until it lay sprawled across the ground with its tongue lolling in the dirt.

"Pippa?" Grassina called softly, but the little snake didn't answer. With the silver wolf at the base of the tree and no idea how far the werewolves had gone, Grassina was reluctant to climb down. It was dark as well, and a bad time to be on foot in the enchanted forest. Wincing at every little sound, Grassina wedged her body in the tree so that even if she fell asleep, she wouldn't fall to the ground, then shut her eyes, hoping that it would be morning when she opened them again.

Fourteen

"Wake up," a voice whispered into her ear, and Grassina's eyes flew open. For the second time she woke to find Pippa staring at her from only inches away.

Grassina squirmed out of the crook in the tree where she'd spent the night. Her muscles were so stiff when she tried to stand that she had to hang on to an overhead branch to haul herself up. "Is the wolf gone?" she asked, remembering why she was in a tree at all.

"Ssee for yoursself," said Pippa.

The little snake twined around her wrist as Grassina peered down through the branches. Instead of the wolf, the beautiful young woman who had been talking to Pippa the day before lay at the foot of the tree. Even in the light of day the woman didn't look quite real. Grassina rubbed her eyes, afraid that she might be hallucinating.

She almost fell out of the tree when the woman yawned and sat up. "You shouldn't be down there!" called

Grassina. Dropping from branch to branch without actually falling, she reached the young woman's side moments later. "Do you know what lives in these woods? You'd better come with me. I'll take you somewhere you can be safe." Grassina offered her hand to the woman, who laughed and pushed it away.

The woman didn't look very old, although certainly older than Grassina. She laughed again when she saw Grassina's earnest expression and patted her shoulder as she might a friendly dog. "You really do care what happens to me!" she said, sounding delighted.

A twig cracked in the forest. For a second, Grassina wondered if the werewolves were coming back.

"I told you she wass a good persson," said Pippa.

"You were right," said the young woman.

Crows took off cawing as if an intruder had startled them. Whatever was coming, Grassina thought it seemed to be getting closer.

"Do you two know each other?" she asked Pippa, feeling oddly betrayed.

"We've met," said the young woman.

Grassina looked at her with growing suspicion. "You aren't Mudine, are you?"

"By the buds of my home tree, no, I'm not a witch!"

"She'ss a Vila," offered Pippa. "She'ss here to protect the foresst and all the creaturess in it."

The Vila nodded. "That's true, and because you

chased away that werewolf for me, I'm going to honor you by making you my blood sister."

Grassina blinked. She could have sworn she'd seen Haywood's face peeking through the leaves behind the Vila, but when she looked again, his face was gone.

"Your what?" she asked. After seeing the wolves trying to tear each other apart the night before, she didn't think she wanted to be a blood anything.

"My blood sister. That means you'll be under my protection and I'll teach you all sorts of wonderful things. I don't offer this opportunity to just anyone, but since you helped me last night—"

"I didn't help you. I've never seen you before!"

The Vila made a trilling sound that reminded Grassina of a songbird. It occurred to her that the Vila was laughing. "Why, of course you helped me! I'll admit I didn't look the way I do now. I looked more like this...." The air around the Vila shimmered and suddenly the young woman was gone, replaced by the silver wolf. The wolf yipped and licked Grassina's hand, then the air shimmered again and the young woman was back, wearing a smug smile.

"Get away from her, Grassina," said Haywood, stepping from behind the tree. "Vili are nothing but trouble, even the ones who claim to be good."

The Vila whirled around to face him. "How dare you!" she shouted. "All I've done is offer to take care of that girl and teach her what she wants to know. Your snake friend told me that you want to learn all about plants," she said, turning to Grassina. "I can teach you everything, far more than some sawed-off stump of a wizard can."

Grassina blanched when she saw the thunderous look on the Vila's face. "But I don't want—"

"You know who I am?" said Haywood.

"I know everything that goes on in my forest." The Vila took a step toward him.

Grassina darted around the Vila, hoping to get between the two of them.

"I even know that you won't make it back alive to that miserable swamp," said the Vila. "Out of my way, child," she told Grassina. "I'm going to see that this young man never taints my forest with his presence again!"

"No!" said Grassina, flinging up her hands as if to push the Vila away. "You can't!"

"Oh, I see how it is. He's a man, and he's used his manly influence on you. Don't worry, I know a cure for *that*! Come over here," the Vila said, taking Grassina's arm in an iron grip and pulling her toward a tree. "I'll turn you into a tree nymph. Then you can live inside the tree and forget all about men and—"

"Let go of me!" cried Grassina. "I don't want to be a tree nymph! I want to be who I am and stay with Haywood!"

"You aren't in love with him, are you?" the Vila asked, looking appalled. "Because if you are, there's no hope for you. If you know what's good for you, you'll reconsider. I would take care of you and teach you everything you ever wanted to know!"

"We can take care of ourselves!" Grassina said, struggling against the Vila. "And I'll learn what I want to know without you. Now let go of me! I mean it. I don't want to go into any tree!"

"Just a minute," said Haywood. "You claim to be the protector of the forest creatures, don't you, Vila?"

"Why, yes, I am," the Vila said, pausing with one hand on the bark of the tree and the other still clutching Grassina's arm.

"Then you won't mind if I invite some of your forest friends to a meal." Raising his voice so that it rang out through the forest, Haywood said,

Termites fast and termites slow,
This is where you'll want to go.
Come and have a tasty treat.
Eat until your meal's complete.
Bring your friends and dig right in.
Hurry so you can begin.

The Vila's head whipped around as the smell of sawdust pervaded the forest. Fallen leaves and other debris on the forest floor rose and fell in waves as a horde of termites left whatever they were eating and scurried toward the tree. "No!" the Vila screamed at the insects. "That's my tree! You can't eat that!"

"But they're forest creatures, too," said Haywood. "And you're supposed to be the champion of all forest creatures, aren't you?"

"Not all of them," cried the Vila. "Just the ones I like. And I don't like termites!" Grassina stumbled when the woman suddenly let go of her arm. While the Vila strode into the midst of the termites, Haywood motioned for Grassina to join him. She was reaching for his hand when the Vila began waving her arms in a shooing motion. A cloud of termites were flung backward through the air, but it made little difference, for the more the Vila tried to get rid of them, the more they poured out of the surrounding forest.

The moment the woman turned her back on them, Haywood began pulling Grassina behind him. "Let's get as far from here as we can before she notices!" he said. Tightening their grip on each other's hands, they ran, their feet slipping on the carpet of skittering insects.

"How did you find me?" Grassina asked as she fought to stay upright.

"When you didn't return to the island last night, I asked if anyone had seen what happened to you. A little bird told me where to look."

Suddenly, a shadow detached itself from the gloom under an ancient tree and stepped into the half-light of the forest directly in their path. "Well, well, now isn't this cozy?" said a tall, thin man with long dark hair. Grassina thought he looked vaguely familiar. With thick eyebrows that met in the middle and long incisors that glinted when he smiled, he looked threatening enough to make her shiver. "If it isn't the little princess who stopped by the village looking for her father."

As more men emerged from the shadows, Haywood turned to Grassina. "Princess?"

She shrugged. "I meant to tell you sometime. Then after a while it no longer seemed important."

"How could your being a princess not be important?"

"I just thought—"

"Excuse me!" interrupted the man. "I was talking, remember?"

Grassina wanted to tell the stranger that he was being rude, but she thought better of it when she saw the oversized knife he was wielding.

Shoving Grassina behind him, Haywood said in a commanding voice, "What's the meaning of this?"

Grassina thought Haywood was incredibly brave for standing up to the man, but when the stranger started toward them, she noticed the scabbed-over gash on his forehead and the blood encrusting his hair. "Uh, Haywood," she said, tugging on his sleeve. "That's not an ordinary man."

"I know that," Haywood said out of the side of his

mouth. "He's a lunatic with bad teeth who is threatening us with a knife."

"That's not what I mean," said Grassina. "I saw him in the village and again last night. He's a werewolf, and I bet those other men are, too."

"A werewolf?" said Haywood. "Are you sure?"

"She's a smart little thing," said the leader, "to figure out who we are."

"That wizard sent termites after the Vila's tree!" said a red-headed man with drooping eyelids. "What do you think he'll do to us, infest our coats with fleas?"

A lean man with a sly face glanced at his companion. "Then he's too late as far as you're concerned. You already have them!" The rest of the men laughed, sounding more like barking dogs than humans.

"Haywood!" whispered Grassina. "We have to do something."

"Give me a minute," he said. "I'm trying to remember what I read about them."

"He wants a minute to think!" said the scruffy man, nudging another in the ribs.

"Then today's his lucky day. He'll have plenty of time to think—while he's taking his eternal rest! Get 'em, boys!" shouted the leader.

"Have you thought of anything yet?" Grassina asked as the men crowded closer.

"Yes, run!" Half pushing, half dragging her, Haywood

hustled Grassina to an ancient oak as big around as a small hut. After boosting her into the lower branches, he turned back, ready to defend her with nothing more than a branch he'd picked up off the ground.

Grassina was digging into her sack for her stones when the men threw themselves at Haywood. He fought valiantly, jabbing and whaling at them with the branch. Grassina was about to throw a stone when the scruffy man grabbed her ankle from behind.

"Let go of me, you . . ." Kicking and shaking her foot, she held on to a sturdy branch with both hands, but the man was stronger, and she knew she couldn't hold on for long. He yanked hard, and she half fell out of the tree, her legs dangling in empty air. Grassina shrieked and tried to kick him, but he ducked and wove, avoiding her blows. She was still struggling to hold on when Pippa's head popped out of Grassina's sleeve. Hissing softly, the little snake dropped onto the man's back.

One more yank and Grassina tumbled to the ground, landing on her side with an *oof*. The man was bending over her when Pippa slithered down the neck of his tunic. "Hey!" he shouted. Letting go of Grassina, he began patting his clothes. "There's a snake! Get this—" The next instant he collapsed in a heap and lay on the ground with saliva dribbling from his mouth. He made gasping sounds while his eyes rolled back in his head.

Grassina scrambled to her feet. "What did you do?" she asked, picking up Pippa.

The little snake curled around her wrist, tickling her skin with a flicking tongue. "The ssame thing he wass going to do to you," said Pippa. "I bit him."

"Are you venomous?" Grassina asked.

"Yess," Pippa said, sounding resigned. "But don't tell anyone. People tend to look at me differently once they know. You sstill like me, don't you?"

"Of course I do," said Grassina. "Just don't . . ."

"You know I'd never bite a friend, but if I'm going to bite more like him, we'll have to wait until I make new venom. I ussed all that I had jusst then. Ssay, maybe your luck hass changed. It wass good luck that I wass there to help you!"

The men on the other side of the tree began barking jubilantly, having overwhelmed Haywood and forced him to the ground. Grassina started toward him, but a trio of men blocked her way. With only two stones left, she threw one at the first of her attackers, hitting him squarely on the forehead. He staggered and went down, but was back on his feet a moment later. The second stone struck another man on the shoulder, which just seemed to make him angry. He snarled, his lips curling like a wolf's.

Grassina studied the forest around her; she was surrounded with no place to go and no one who could help.

Looking for a weapon of some sort, she snatched a stick off the ground and held it out in front of her. "I wish I had a real weapon," she said. "Something that would work against werewolves!"

She nearly dropped the stick when it began to shiver in her hand, but she held on, as mesmerized by the light that came from it as were the men who slowed down to watch. The stick grew until it was the length of a spear, its tip becoming thick and pointed. When it stopped quivering, the glow burst into a silvery radiance that banished the half-light of the forest.

In the full light of day, the men rushed at Grassina, brandishing knives and daggers. Holding the spear as she'd seen her father's soldiers do, she hurled it as hard as she could at the man in the lead. Although her aim was off, the spear righted itself and flew directly at him. It struck, the tip slicing deep, the shaft quivering as the man fell. Grassina was defenseless now, but only for a moment as the spear slid back out of the motionless figure, rose into the air, and returned to her hand. She glanced at the fallen man, half dreading, half hoping to see that she had killed him. To her surprise, he had been infused with a silvery glow, not unlike that of the spear.

As Grassina watched, the man shuddered, and when he lay still again, all signs that he had ever been a werewolf were gone. His long incisors had grown smaller, his bushy brow had shrunk, and even his demeanor had changed. The werewolf part of him was gone, yet when he stirred and sat up, Grassina could see that his human aspect still lived.

A twig snapped behind her, and Grassina spun around. The remaining men were circling her, made wary by the spear. Grassina hefted it and took aim, throwing the spear when a man launched himself at her. It struck as truly as if she'd been a seasoned fighter, taking him out of the fray. Then, just as before, the spear flew back to her hand while the injured werewolf became fully human.

Poised for another attack, Grassina turned and drew back her spear. Having seen what had happened to their comrades, the men who were still on their feet seemed to have lost all interest in her. Even as they slunk away, Grassina hurried to find Haywood and discovered him lying sprawled on the ground, bleeding badly and barely alive.

"No!" she said, kneeling down beside him. "You can't die! Haywood, I need you!"

"He doesn't have to die," said a voice. Grassina looked up and saw the Vila.

"Can you save him?" Grassina asked. "Surely there is something you can do. . . ."

"You don't need me," said the Vila. "You have magic of your own."

"What are you talking about?"

"How do you think you got the weapon you needed when you needed it the most?" the Vila asked.

"You mean you didn't send me the spear?" Grassina glanced down at the gleaming pole she still clutched in her hand.

The Vila shook her head. "You did that all on your own. Try a healing spell. It should work."

"But I don't know how!" wailed Grassina.

"Just as I doubt you knew how to throw a spear. Try it and see. The magic will do the hard part for you."

"I don't know any healing spells."

"You must. Haven't you ever seen an injury healed through magic?"

"I did fall out of a tree once; my mother healed my broken arm."

"Good. Then think back," said the Vila, laying her cool, dry palm on Grassina's forehead.

"I don't really remember. . . . Wait. Yes, I think that's it. I'll have to change it a little, but I think it went something like this."

> Bones may break and flesh may tear.
> Neither one's beyond repair.
> Bones and flesh and sinew, too.
> With this spell make them like new.
> Mend the one I love so well.
> Use my love to aid this spell.

Haywood groaned and moved his head ever so slightly, but otherwise nothing happened. "It didn't work!" cried Grassina. "Now what am I going to do?"

"It didn't work because you don't love him enough," said the Vila.

"But you said yourself that I love him!"

The Vila sighed. "I'm not saying you don't, just not enough to make that spell work. However, I can assist with that if you'd like. You helped me when I needed it, and I have yet to repay you. I don't like feeling obligated to anyone, even someone who rejected the offer of sisterhood."

"I'd appreciate anything you can do if it will help Haywood."

The Vila nodded. Waving her hands over Grassina and Haywood, she said something in a language Grassina didn't understand.

"What was that?"

"A love enhancement spell. It works only when two people are learning to love each other. Your healing spell should work now."

"Thank you," breathed Grassina. Turning back to Haywood, she was surprised to see that he didn't look exactly the same as he had before. She thought he was handsomer now and so appealing that her heart ached at how helpless he looked. Eager to see the healing spell's effect, she repeated it all in one breath, then held her next breath as she waited to see if it would work.

The forest seemed unnaturally quiet, as if every creature wanted to see what would happen. Haywood took a
ragged breath and then another. As color flushed his pale
cheeks and his wounds began to heal before her eyes,
Grassina took his hand in hers and squeezed it.

Haywood opened his eyes in response, smiling up at
her when he saw her bending close. At first delighted by
his smile, Grassina drew back when his incisors began to
grow and a feral light filled his eyes.

"I was afraid of that," said the Vila. "It looks as if he's
turning into a werewolf now that he isn't going to die.
You don't have any choice. You'll have to take your spear
and stab him."

Grassina was horrified. "I can't do that!"

"Of course you can. Think about what happened
to those werewolves you struck with the spear. The spell
didn't kill their human side, just the werewolf in them. It
will do the same for your young man if you let it."

"What are you talking about?" Haywood asked, propping himself on his elbows.

"Nothing," said the Vila. "Now hold still while she
pokes you. It won't hurt . . . much. No worse than a thorn
prick."

Haywood jumped to his feet. "No one's stabbing me
with a spear! You have to be crazy if you think . . ."

"Will it really work?" Grassina asked the Vila.

"I'm certain it will," said the Vila.

"I'm sorry, love of my life, but I must do this," Grassina told Haywood.

Haywood began backing away. "Oh no, you don't! Whatever she's told you, my darling, whatever I've done, I'm sure we can work this out."

"We'll talk all about it," said Grassina, "as soon as you're no longer a werewolf."

"I'm not a werewolf," Haywood growled.

"Yes, you are. Feel how long your teeth have grown. Your eyebrows meet in the middle now, although they didn't before. And you're beginning to smell like a dog."

Haywood continued to back away. "I admit I haven't bathed recently, but that's no reason to . . ."

"Now!" shouted the Vila as Haywood tripped over her outstretched foot.

Grassina stabbed him in the leg as gently as she could. Haywood gasped and began to struggle upright, but the light infused him just as the spear sprang back into Grassina's hand, and he collapsed again.

"That should do it," said the Vila.

"I thought you were certain it would!"

"I am . . . fairly certain," the Vila said as Haywood continued to lie motionless at their feet.

"Haywood!" Grassina cried, falling on her knees beside him. "My sweet, sweet darling! Light of my life, what have I done?" Bending over him, Grassina kissed him full on the lips.

"That was very nice, precious love," Haywood muttered against her mouth, "but can you please get up? You're kneeling on my hand."

Grassina sat back on her heels and clasped her hands together. "Oh, Haywood, you're all right!"

"Uh, yes," he said, flexing his fingers. "Thanks to you, my darling doodlebug."

Grassina frowned and turned to the Vila. "We've never called each other silly names before. What have you done to us?"

"Nothing that wouldn't have happened anyway, given a little time. You were already in love. I just made your love stronger. No spell can create love if there is none to begin with, but because of my spell, you will love each other for the rest of your days as long as you remain in the form you have now. However, if you ever get tired of it, just come see me. I can always turn you into a tree nymph, and then you'd forget all about him."

"I'll never tire of my dearest Haywood," said Grassina.

"Then in that case there's no need to thank me!"

Fifteen

They were sitting by the fire in front of Haywood's half-built hut when Grassina told him about her family. "And so Chartreuse said that she hated me and never wanted to see me again," she continued. "I left the next morning and don't ever want to go back." The last log cracked in two, showering sparks into the night air. A sleepy bird protested from its nest in one of the plum trees. Grassina leaned against Haywood's leg. "I could stay here with you, heart's delight. Between your magic and mine, we could be safe and very comfortable. There's no need for either of us to leave."

"That would be a dream come true, my treasure," Haywood said, caressing her fingers where they lay across his palm. "But I don't think it's possible. I need you, and I want you here with me, but I think Greater Greensward needs you more right now."

"You'd send me away?" she asked.

"Not because I want to. I love you, dearest darling.

I have ever since you built that terrible hut and were too proud to ask for help. You're the bravest girl I've ever met and the most understanding. Nothing would make me happier than to have you here with me for the rest of my life. Ordinarily, I wouldn't be able to say these things to you— you being a princess and me the younger son of a minor noble—but I think you love me as much as I love you—"

"Oh, I do, light of my life," breathed Grassina. "I have never felt about anyone the way I feel about you. I'll stay with you and we can use our magic to build a bigger home, by the river perhaps, or—"

"As much as I want that, it wouldn't be right. The kingdom needs you, precious one. Go back to your castle and see if your sister has her magic yet and if it's enough to return things to the way they were. Whatever happens, come back to me. I'll be waiting for you here."

Grassina sighed heavily. "I suppose I have to go. I thought when I ran away that my duty to Greater Greensward was over, but I guess that's never going to happen. I'll be responsible to the kingdom forever."

"All princesses are born into responsibility. There's no getting around that."

"Then stay safe while I'm gone, light of my life. I'll leave in the morning and be back as soon as I can. If you need me for any reason . . ."

"I'll send a little bird," said Haywood. "But I'm sure I'll be fine. The werewolves aren't likely to follow us here.

It's you I'm worried about. Your mother will still be the same."

"Yes, but now she won't be the only one with magic. Somehow the thought of seeing her isn't quite so daunting. I just wish I felt the same about seeing Chartreuse."

❧

Going home felt odd, mostly because nothing seemed to have changed since the morning she'd left. The same men were standing guard at the drawbridge, looking bored and only half awake. The same cats were scrapping with bristled backs and puffed tails in front of the stable doors. The Great Hall still smelled of the old herbs that needed to be replaced, the hounds sleeping in front of the cold hearth, and the unwashed bodies of the people who passed through. Grassina almost felt as if she'd never left, yet too many things had happened to her, changing her in ways she never would have expected.

She was trying to decide if she should go look for her mother or her sister first when she heard Olivene's unmistakable screech. "I don't know why you had to show up! I was just getting used to you being gone! My life was nice and peaceful without you. Why did you have to spoil it by coming back?"

At first Grassina thought her mother was talking to her, but the queen was nowhere in sight. Following the sound of Olivene's voice, Grassina found her by the stairs leading into the dungeon. A pile of her father's belongings had been heaped beside the door, shrinking steadily as Olivene snatched one object after another and chucked it down the stairs. "Here, take this!" screamed the queen. "No one else wants your trash!"

"Mother?" said Grassina. "What are you doing?"

Olivene's head whipped around. "Oh, it's you. So you decided to come back from wherever you've been hiding. I don't know why you bothered. We don't need you here."

Grassina shrugged. "In that case, I'll be going," she said, glancing toward the door to the courtyard.

"You most certainly will not!" said Olivene. "Here, take this. See how hard you can throw it. If you do it right, it should bounce all the way down the stairs."

Grassina took the sword from her mother's gnarled hands. It was her father's best sword, the one he'd worn during every important ceremony. She glanced at the pile. His armor was there, as were his books, his clothes, and even the dishes he'd used in the Great Hall. "What's going on, Mother?" asked Grassina.

"I'll tell you what," said the queen. "Your father came back the night before last. He came to see me the last time I went down there. As if anyone wants to see *him* again."

"My father? How can that be? You mean he didn't really die?" Grassina asked, hope lighting her eyes.

"He died all right. I never said he didn't. He's still dead, too, so don't start thinking there's been some sort of miracle. He's come back as a ghost, determined to haunt me for the rest of my days. You couldn't leave well enough alone, could you, you miserable old cuss?" Olivene shouted down the stairs.

"Has Chartreuse seen him?" Grassina asked, thinking her mother was imagining things.

"That ninny? Ha! She refuses to go down there. Says she doesn't believe in ghosts. That's a whole lot of hooey if you ask me. She's just afraid; I can see it in her eyes."

"She was very upset when he died."

"Not enough to go see him now that he's back! You should visit him though. I'm sure the old stick would like to see you. Here, take this. I don't want the darn thing getting stuck in the stairwell." Grassina had to set the sword on the floor to take the armored breastplate that her mother was handing to her. She thought she saw tears glinting in her mother's eyes, but she couldn't be certain. The queen turned away too quickly, saying, "You can take the rest of this junk down there while you're at it. I don't want it cluttering up the place anymore. I'll throw it out if he doesn't want it."

"Are you sure . . . ," Grassina began, but her mother was already stomping off.

Gathering as many of her father's possessions as she could carry, Grassina picked her way down the stairs, trying not to step on the clutter Olivene had tossed there. Beady rat eyes watched her from the open doorways of some of the cells, but the only sound was that of her own feet on the stone floor. Remembering the ghosts she'd met before, she kept her eyes open for any sign of what her father might have become, but the dungeon was unusually quiet. Grassina had begun to wonder if her mother had finally slipped over the edge into insanity when she reached the door to the room her father had used.

Grassina wasn't sure if she wanted to see him there or not. Although she missed him desperately, it was the man she missed, not some disembodied wraith who floated through walls and spoke in half whispers. But when she saw a familiar shape limned in blue, though it was little more than a shadow in the flickering light of the torch in the corridor, her heart skipped a beat and she felt an overwhelming sense of relief. Her father was back, in whatever form, and now everything would be all right.

"Father, is that you?" Grassina asked from the doorway.

The figure turned around with shadows rippling on shadows. "Grassina, my darling girl," said a whispery voice as the figure drifted closer. "Your mother told me that you were gone. 'Ran away,' she said. She was making it up, of course."

"I was gone, Father, but I'm back now."

The ghost approached until Grassina could make out her father's features. Despite his hollow eye sockets and skin of palest blue, it was most definitely her father. He was so transparent that she could see the walls and broken furniture behind him, but he was there, or at least some part of him was, and just then that was enough. Grassina shivered as the ghost came closer with arms outstretched and a gentle smile on his face. She expected to be enveloped in a chilly hug, but the ghost passed right through her. Grassina felt woozy the way she did when she stood up too fast, although this was much worse. The experience left her cold, shaky, and slightly queasy.

"That was very odd," said her father, "and most unexpected." His outline wavered as if he were shuddering.

Grassina rubbed the goose bumps that had risen on her arms. "I know what you mean."

"I must apologize, my dear," said her father. "I'm not used to being a ghost and have yet to learn what I can and cannot do. In my joy at seeing you again, I forgot that I can't actually touch physical objects."

"I understand," Grassina muttered from behind her hand. Her stomach was roiling, but she didn't want to talk about it.

"I'd like to be able to write, or read what others have written, but I can neither hold a quill nor turn the pages."

"Maybe I can help you with that," said Grassina. "I can do the writing for you and turn the pages when you're ready. But we'll have to put this room to rights first. Mother certainly made a shambles of things. Just a minute while I set these over here." Grassina placed the items she'd brought in the corner of the room while her father hovered beside her. Brushing off her hands, she glanced at him, then at the pile of armor and clothing. "If you can't touch anything, I don't know what Mother expects you to do with all this."

"I don't think she knows either. I believe it's her way of telling me that she loves me. She doesn't know how to say it anymore, but I know in my heart," he said, pointing at his chest, "how she really feels. It's why I had to come back, and it's why I can't leave."

Her father had never had much in the room, so it didn't take long for Grassina to straighten it up. The larger furniture had been broken into pieces, making them easier to cram through the doorway, and the rest was light enough that she could move it on her own. After setting the sheets of parchment in two stacks that she could organize later, she folded his clothes and replaced them in the not-too-badly damaged trunk. "I'll bring everything else down now," she said, heading toward the door. "Mother has quite a pile up there. She'll throw it out if I don't move it."

"Then by all means," said King Aldrid. "I wouldn't want to upset your mother."

❧

Grassina loaded her arms with as much as she could carry for the next two trips, but her father's armor was heavy, and she couldn't carry more than a few pieces at a time. As she was setting his helmet on the pile, she knocked over his shield, which fell on the arch of her foot. She howled and dropped the rest on the floor, hobbling to the only chair in the room so she could inspect the injury. No skin was broken, but her foot hurt almost as much as the time a horse had stepped on it.

"Why don't you rest for a moment?" said her father, floating in the air above her. "You can tell me about what you've been up to."

"There's a lot to tell," said Grassina.

Her father chuckled—a hollow sound that would have been frightening if Grassina hadn't known who made it. "I have nothing but time," he said. "You can begin with the day you left the castle."

Relieved that she wouldn't have to talk about his death, Grassina rubbed her aching foot and told him about her fight with Chartreuse. She described her feeling of hopelessness and how she'd left the castle before first light. Her father was intrigued when she told him about Pippa, and asked countless questions when she mentioned Haywood. When she described the Vila, he grew restless, becoming even more agitated when she talked about the werewolves. "You could have been killed!"

"And I would have been if the spear hadn't appeared in my hand. I came into my magic, Father! Just when I needed it most!"

"You what?" said King Aldrid, his color flaring a brighter blue.

"I thought the Vila had sent the spear to me, but later when I had to stab Haywood, she told me she hadn't."

King Aldrid's ghost seemed to shrink as he settled to the floor. "This is too much for me to take in all at once. You have magic? Wait . . . Why would you stab your friend?"

"So he wouldn't stay a werewolf," said Grassina. When her father seemed even more confused, she explained it all as best she could, although she left out the part about the Vila's love enhancement spell. Even without the spell, she was sure she would have loved Haywood, but she didn't feel like explaining that to her father.

"And so I came home to see if I'm needed here. I'm sure I won't be if Chartreuse has come into her magic. . . . You haven't heard anything about that, have you?"

Her father sighed and shook his head. "Your mother hasn't come back down since she first discovered that I was here, and I haven't seen or heard from your sister."

"Then as soon as I finish bringing everything, I'll see if I can find her. I know she won't want to see me, but this isn't about what either of us wants."

"You don't have to carry the rest down yourself. Use your magic. It would be much faster and easier for you."

"Oh," said Grassina. It hadn't occurred to her that she could use her magic for anything but an emergency. The thought of reciting a spell to perform such an ordinary task made her look at her magic differently—making it less of a weapon and more of a tool. As far as she knew, there was no reason she couldn't use it for all sorts of things the way her mother had.

"That's a good idea," said Grassina. "Only I don't know any spells for moving things. I don't think I ever heard Mother mention one to Chartreuse."

King Aldrid shrugged. "Then make one up. Your mother always did."

᳇

Grassina stood at the top of the stairs, poking the pile of clothes and weapons with the foot that wasn't sore. It had sounded good to say that she could make up a spell, but now that she was faced with the task of actually doing it, she had no idea where to begin. She debated telling her father that it wouldn't work, then decided that it wouldn't hurt to try. Clearing her throat, Grassina pointed at the pile and said,

> Carry this from here to there.
> Haul it down the dungeon stair.
> Take it to the tiny room
> Where my father met his doom.

A fly landed on the pile, tasting the old leather of the undercoat that her father had worn beneath his chain mail. Grassina was beginning to think that she'd done something wrong when the pile seemed to quiver, then collapsed, disappearing in a nearly silent whoosh and taking the fly with it.

"It worked!" she said, delighted with herself as well as the knowledge that she wouldn't have to carry everything down the stairs.

"It certainly did!" crowed her mother behind her. "You have your magic! I should have known you'd be the one!"

Grassina twirled to face Olivene, too elated about her magic to feel nervous around her mother. "Did you see that? Wasn't it wonderful?" Her smile faded when she saw that her sister was there as well, looking as angry as she'd ever seen her.

"Simply marvelous," said Chartreuse in a flat, tight voice. "It was some kind of trick, wasn't it? You don't really have magic; you just want us to believe you do so we'll forget that you ran off the way you did. First Clarence goes off to fight a dragon and gets himself killed, then Pietro disappears. They say he went to find the Vila. He never could resist a pretty face. And then you ran away, leaving me desperately afraid that something awful had happened to you, too. Don't you think I care about you? You're the only sister I have. And you know I need you here. Greater Greensward needs you here. I can't handle *everything* myself!"

"Don't be such a sourpuss, Chartreuse," said Olivene. "You'll make a competent queen, but you'll never be the

Green Witch. Just because you can't do it doesn't mean that your sister can't. I saw her do it with my own two eyes and so did you. I've been sorely disappointed in you, Chartreuse, but now I know why you never came into your magic. It wasn't in you and it never will be. Magic runs true in our family—goes to the most deserving, I'd say. Does your father know, Grassina? I'm going to go tell him."

While Olivene thumped down the stairs, Chartreuse glared at her sister, standing with her feet firmly planted and her fists on her hips. "I bet you're proud of yourself and think you're really special," said Chartreuse. "Well, you're not. Look at your hand. If your magic was as good as Mother seems to think it is, you'd have the Green Witch's ring on your finger. Don't try lording your magic over me, miss. The ability to do a few simple tricks doesn't impress me. Mother will see soon enough what you can do. And there's no saying I won't still get my magic, and then we'll see who's better at it!"

Grassina put up her hand as if to stop the flow of words. "Chartreuse, I—"

Chartreuse shook her head. "I don't want to talk to you, so do us both a favor and don't say another word. But while you practice your magic or whatever it is you're going to go do, keep in mind that I'm not the only one with a responsibility to the people of this kingdom!"

Sixteen

Grassina sat on the edge of her bed staring at the wall across from her. She hated to admit that Chartreuse was right, but it looked like this time she was. It hadn't occurred to Grassina until her sister mentioned it that she might have earned the Green Witch's ring if her magic had been strong enough. With the ring on her finger, she would know that she was capable of protecting the kingdom however necessary. Without the ring, Grassina wasn't sure that she could protect much of anything.

After Chartreuse's tirade, Grassina had fled to her room, hoping that even if the ring wasn't on her finger, the tapestry might have appeared on her wall. It hadn't been there, of course; she hadn't really expected that it would be. Now it was even clearer that there still was no Green Witch to protect Greater Greensward.

It had been only one day since she'd returned to the castle and it already felt like an eternity. Nothing was the way it had been. Her mother was making Chartreuse do all the chores. Chartreuse hadn't spoken a word to Grassina since they'd met outside the dungeon door, which was probably just as well.

It didn't help that Grassina missed Haywood dreadfully and thought about him all the time, or that worrying about the ring had kept her from sleeping most of the night. All the next day, she'd drifted through the castle, unsettled and unsure about what she should be doing. By late afternoon, she'd once again returned to her room to stare at the empty wall.

Grassina was still sitting on her bed when she heard someone sobbing. Opening her door, she peeked out and found Lettie, the scullery maid, crying. "What's wrong?" Grassina asked.

Lettie's face was even redder than usual, and her cheeks were streaked with tears. "Oh, Your Highness," she wailed, "I didn't want to disturb you, but I don't know who else to turn to. They say you helped that man from Darby-in-the-Woods, so I was hoping you could help me, too."

"Are you having a problem with werewolves?" asked Grassina.

"Yes! Well, not me exactly. My Basil is a soldier. He was on patrol last night, and he went missing along with some of his friends. He told me he'd be safe enough— they weren't going beyond sight of the castle—but he never came back, and I think the werewolves got him!

What am I to do, Your Highness? He was just about to propose to me, I know he was!"

"I wish I could help, but I don't know what I could do. I'm not the Green Witch," said Grassina, holding up her ringless hand.

"And your mother isn't either! We've all seen that she's lost the ring, and everyone knows that Princess Chartreuse hasn't a magic bone in her body. Everyone's saying that it's you who has the magic now, so I thought . . ."

"I'm sorry, I'm not the one to do this. You'll have to find someone else," Grassina said, pulling the door closed behind her.

Turning toward her bed, Grassina paused, her hand still on the latch. She could hear Lettie sobbing as she retreated down the corridor, and Grassina couldn't blame her. There wasn't anyone else, and everyone knew it. Ever since she'd faced the werewolves in the forest, she'd been hoping she'd never see them again. She'd even harbored the unlikely thought that they could have left altogether, scared off by the power of her spear. However, deep down inside she'd known this wasn't true; it was the reason she'd been awake most of the night. Ridding the kingdom of the werewolves was going to be up to her, for even her small bit of magic was more than anyone else who cared seemed to have.

"Perhaps Father has some advice," she murmured, squaring her shoulders as she turned back to the door.

She found King Aldrid exactly where she'd seen him last, drifting silently in the darkened room. He seemed to be as lost as she had felt since her return. "I need your help," she said, plunking herself down on the only chair. It wobbled on its cracked leg, so she hopped off and sat on the trunk instead. Seeing the stack of parchments on the floor, she remembered her offer to help with his writing and to turn the pages so he could read—yet another thing only she seemed able to do.

Her father's ghost sighed. "I don't know how much help I can give you. I can't even go upstairs."

"Really?" said Grassina. "You mean you've tried?"

King Aldrid nodded. "I think it's because I have no substance. I can go through walls and doors, but I can't climb the steps. I pass right through them, too."

"There must be something you can do."

"I'm sure there's a trick to it," he said, rubbing his ghostly chin. "I'll just have to keep trying. Now, you said you needed my help?"

Grassina nodded. "It's the werewolves. They're coming as close as the castle. Some of our guards are missing."

"That's bad," said the king. "Very bad. But there isn't anything I can do."

"I know," said Grassina. "I'm going to handle it myself. All I want from you is advice on how to get rid of them. What do werewolves fear? Is there anything special I can use to chase them off?"

"Silver," he said promptly. "A silver-tipped arrow lodged firmly in the heart should do the trick."

"But there are so many of them, and I'm just one person. I can't possibly shoot them all. Isn't there anything else I can use?"

"Silver-tipped arrows are the most effective weapon that I've ever employed, although I suppose if you cut off the werewolves' heads . . ."

Grassina shuddered. She was willing to fight them if she had to, but she couldn't imagine cutting off anyone's head. "Thank you, Father," she said, getting to her feet. "I'll be sure to keep that in mind."

Something crashed in a nearby cell, and Olivene shrieked wordlessly. "Has Mother started coming to the dungeon again?" asked Grassina.

"Since yesterday," said her father's ghost. "We talked about your magic. She's very proud of you, although I think she's being a bit hard on Chartreuse."

"I'd help Chartreuse if I could," said Grassina.

"As would I," said the king. "I just need to find a way out of here."

"I think I'll go talk to Mother and see if she has any suggestions about the werewolves," said Grassina.

"She might," said the king. "Although I don't know if you should do *anything* she says."

Grassina found her mother standing on top of a pitted green leather trunk, hanging bird skeletons from the ceiling. "Oh, it's you," she said when Grassina appeared in the doorway. "Hand me that grackle. No, not that one, the one with the chipped beak. Good. Now, what do you want? I know you didn't come to watch me redecorate. Speak up. I'm busy. No time for idle chitchat."

Grassina ducked to avoid the skeleton of a raven. "I've come to ask you about werewolves. Do you have anything that I could use to get rid of them?"

Olivene guffawed, opening her mouth wide enough to show the gaps between her blackened, rotting teeth. "You make those werewolves sound like fleas in your underthings," she finally said. "Any way to get rid of them? Hah! Watch out, that buzzard is coming after you." Grassina jumped out of the way as one of the larger skeletons clipped her shoulder with its wing. She scowled at the bird, who looked as if it were scowling back. "Werewolves, huh?" Olivene continued. "I've never had much to do with them. Why are you asking?"

"I told you about the werewolves in the enchanted forest. They're still there and are moving this way. Would you like to take care of them, or should I?" Grassina asked, still hoping that she wouldn't have to be the one to face them.

"Is that a trick question? Because I don't like trick questions, unless I ask them myself. Can't you see that I'm busy? If I don't get all these hung, they'll fly into a tizzy and get their bones mixed up. Hey, don't hurt that raven! Do you know how long it took to get it up there?"

The raven skeleton had grabbed hold of Grassina's braid with its claws and was trying to fly off with it, but it could only circle around the point on the ceiling from which it hung. Grassina took hold of her braid and yanked, pulling it free and bringing three of the bird's claws with it.

"I know what you need," Olivene said, snapping her fingers. Hopping off the trunk, she threw the lid open and began rummaging inside. "Here, take these." Removing a bundle of stiff gray hairs tied with a silver thread, she pulled out two and handed them to Grassina. "They're werewolf whiskers, good for tracking anything within fifty miles. If you're going to use them to track werewolves, do it at night. They won't do you a bit of good otherwise. And this is a witch's tooth that . . . Wait, that's mine. So that's where it went," she said, jamming the blackened bit of bone into her gums. "Then there's this . . . No, I might need it. And this . . . Isn't it a ghastly color? I think I'll keep that. Ah, here you go. I suppose you could have one of these, seeing that I have an extra." Olivene handed Grassina a ridged tooth at least two inches long dangling from a golden chain.

"What is it?" Grassina asked, watching it twirl.

Instead of answering, Olivene scuttled across the floor and tossed the basket of lightning bugs to Grassina. "You might as well take these, too. They're of no use to me, and I'm sick of their infernal din. Now get out! You've taken up too much of my time as it is. So long, good riddance, and all those other things you're supposed to say when an idiot is staring at you big-eyed and jaw-dropped like you are. Shut the door on the way out. I don't want any more unwelcome visitors taking advantage of my good nature."

Although her hands were full, Grassina managed to close the door behind her. The visit hadn't been at all what she'd expected, but then, she didn't have any idea what to expect when she saw her mother. Having set the angrily buzzing basket on the floor, she tucked the were-wolf hairs and the tooth in the sack she carried. At least now she had a few things that she might be able to use, even if her mother had neglected to tell her how.

Seventeen

It was almost dusk when she found Haywood squatting beside the fire, feeding the flames with kindling. A filleted fish lay on a rock beside a pot of water. "I was hoping you'd come back today, my sweet precious, at least to tell me how things were going," he said after they greeted each other with a kiss. "Would you like some fish stew? It won't take long."

"I'm too nervous to eat," Grassina replied. Then she sat down to tell him what she had done and why she had come back when she did. Haywood nodded but didn't interrupt, for which Grassina was grateful. Telling him about her family and the werewolves was already hard enough. "But I think I'll need your help," she said when she'd finished. "You know things about magic that I don't. Together we might know enough to make this work."

Haywood took her hand in his and squeezed it. "I'd go in your stead if I could, but I know my magic isn't strong enough to defeat a pack of werewolves. And your magic hasn't been fully tested. I'm not sure if our magic combined—"

"It has to be," said Grassina. "Someone has to deal with them before the kingdom is overrun. They're getting bolder all the time. They've already been seen near the castle. It won't be long before they turn one of our own men into a werewolf and get inside the castle, too. Greater Greensward needs us, my darling. There isn't time to waste. I'll be leaving as soon as it gets dark. The werewolf whiskers Mother gave me to track them will work only at night."

"And your father . . ."

"He can't help us. He doesn't even know how to help himself yet. And my mother isn't interested, although to be frank, if she were, she might side with the werewolves instead of us. It really is up to you and me."

Haywood sighed and got to his feet. "Let me get my things. I'll be ready in just a minute."

"You mean you'll come?" asked Grassina, her eyes shining.

"Of course. I would never let you do this by yourself."

❧

Grassina collected her spear and was leaving the hut that Haywood had finished in her absence when Pippa wriggled through the interwoven branches, landing on the ground in front of her. "What are you doing here?" Grassina asked, startled.

"Making ssure that you don't leave me behind again. You have a habit of doing that."

"Sorry. I didn't dare take you to the castle. It would have been too hard to hide you from my mother."

"I'll forgive you thiss time," said Pippa. "At leasst I had Haywood for company. Did you know that he'ss very good at finding mice?"

"I thought you looked a little plumper."

"Are you almost ready?" Haywood called from the head of the path. "It's nearly dark out."

"We're both coming," Grassina replied as she picked up the little snake. "We have one more weapon to take with us. Pippa wants to go, too."

᠁

The stars were shining overhead as they neared the edge of the forest. Grassina reached into her sack, took out the whiskers, and held them up to the light of Haywood's witches' ball.

"These are the werewolf whiskers that Mother gave me," she said. "They don't look like much, do they?" She turned them over in her hand and bit her lip while she thought. "Do you have any idea what to do with them? Mother forgot to tell me."

Haywood shrugged. "I've never seen anyone do tracking magic. Have you?"

"It wasn't included in my deportment lessons. I don't

know if Mother ever showed Chartreuse either. I guess I'll have to make up something again. I hate doing this, but here goes."

Holding the hairs on the palm of her hand, Grassina thought for a minute, then said,

> As a bird flies to its nest
> And a fox runs to its den,
> Show us where the werewolves are—
> The wolves now, not the men.

"I hope it workss," said Pippa. "That wass really awful."

"Don't be so critical," said Grassina. "I'm new at this, remember?"

"Look," said Haywood. "They're changing color."

At first it was difficult to see in the flickering light of the torch, but it soon became obvious that the whiskers were turning red. Before long they were glowing a brilliant scarlet. Rising into the air, they rotated until they were both pointing in the same direction, and then they took off like two flaming arrows.

"Hurry!" shouted Grassina, sprinting after the whiskers. "I don't have any more. If we lose sight of those, we'll never find the werewolves!"

"Too bad you didn't usse one at a time!" Pippa said into her ear.

"Don't you think I know that now?" puffed Grassina.

"Save your breath for running," said Haywood. "Look, they're over that ravine."

While Haywood slid down the steep incline, Grassina picked her way more carefully, grabbing hold of branches and crouching when she slipped. Haywood had almost reached the top of the other side when he saw two glowing lines waiting just above his head. He was reaching for Grassina's hand to help her out of the ravine when the whiskers took off again.

"They went that way!" Grassina shouted, stumbling when Haywood jerked her toward him and started running.

Concentrating on keeping up with the racing red streaks, running without regard to being stealthy or quiet, Grassina and Haywood soon forgot why they were running. They kept going until their lungs burned and they had stabbing pains in their sides. They ran until they thought they couldn't run anymore, then they stopped thinking and just put one foot in front of the other. When the whiskers finally grew still and hovered over the remains of a fallen log, Grassina and Haywood didn't notice at first and nearly stumbled past them. In the distance, the full moon rising behind the castle showed them exactly how far they had gone.

"Do you see . . . the werewolves?" Grassina asked, gasping for air.

"Is that . . . them . . . by those rocks?" Haywood whispered back, pointing beyond the last of the trees at a jumble of boulders. A shape moved, jumping onto the tallest rock so that the body was silhouetted against the night sky. Larger than an ordinary wolf, the creature was more muscular as well, as if he were a throwback to a beast of an earlier age that had required greater size and strength to survive.

When the werewolf turned his head and looked directly at them, Grassina whispered, "He knows we're here! Look, the others are spreading out. They'll surround us if they can!"

"If we could keep them together somehow . . . ," said Haywood.

"That gives me an idea," said Grassina, "but I'm going to need your help." Unwrapping the blanket she had wrapped around the basket of lightning bugs, she set it on the ground and stepped back.

"What is that?" asked Haywood.

"Some very angry insects," said Grassina. "You're good at controlling birds and such. Can you tell these bugs to circle around the werewolves and draw them together?"

"Now *that* I can do," said Haywood. Flexing his fingers, he pointed at the basket and murmured something under his breath. "Go!" he said in a louder voice and kicked the basket over.

As the lid fell off, the angrily buzzing swarm of lightning bugs hopped, skittered, crawled, and flew straight at the pack, shedding sparks along the way. The lone were-wolf poised atop the pile of boulders leapt to the ground and began padding toward Grassina and Haywood. The first lightning bugs hit him in the chest, shocking him so that he fell back, whining and snapping at his fur. Other werewolves tried to bypass their stricken leader until the bugs flew at their eyes and they, too, were driven back. Bugs hopped into their open mouths and crawled over their paws, shooting sparks and shocking them at each point of contact. With sparks lighting the way, the light-ning bugs herded the werewolves back toward the rocks. Even after they'd rounded up the entire pack, the bugs continued to shoot off sparks so that it looked like an in-visible fire was burning in the forest.

While Haywood strode purposefully toward the pack of werewolves, Grassina followed with her spear poised to throw, just in case.

"What have you done?" snarled the werewolf who had watched them from the rocks. "Get these things away from us now or I'll rip out your throat!"

"Isn't that what you plan to do anyway?" Grassina asked.

"You understood it?" asked Haywood. "What did it say?"

"I suppose you have to have been an animal to under-stand one," said Grassina. "Maybe you can try being one someday. The beast was threatening us, that's all." Turning back to the werewolf, she pointed her spear at him, saying, "Your threats mean little to me. I can kill you whenever I choose. However, if you promise to leave this kingdom, I'll let you go on the condition that you never come back."

"Leave the . . . Have those insects crawled through your ear holes and infested your brain? We're not making any deals with you! You're a human and nothing more. When I get past these pests . . ." The werewolf swatted at a lightning bug and yelped when it shocked him. Swiping at his paw with his tongue, the werewolf glared at Grassina. "I'll find a way to get around these bugs. When I do, I'll eat your heart while it's still beating."

"Grasssina," Pippa whispered into her ear. "Bad luck. I think that sspell iss wearing off."

"What spell? You mean . . . Oh!" Although the lightning bugs had formed a flashing, sparking wall only moments before, large gaps were beginning to appear as insects deserted one after the other, called away by the clear night sky and the temptations of the forest floor.

The head of the werewolf pack was still watching them when Grassina whispered to Haywood, telling him about the spell. "That's one thing about my kind of magic," replied Haywood as they both backed away. "You can't go against a creature's nature if you want the spell to last. They are only insects after all. We can't really expect them to act like anything else for long."

"I wish you'd told me this before!" said Grassina. "Can't you repeat your spell?"

"I could, but it wouldn't do anything. My spells never work a second time on the same batch of animals."

Grassina frowned and reached into the leather bag. "I suppose I could try this," she said, pulling out the tooth on the chain.

"What kind of animal did that come from?" asked Haywood.

"I was hoping that you could tell me."

Haywood shrugged. "I've never seen anything like it, but whatever it was it must have been big. Look at the size of that thing."

"I hope it was mean, too," said Grassina. "Mean enough to take on a pack of werewolves. But I guess we're about to find out. Here goes." Holding the tooth at arm's length, Grassina said,

> Use this tooth to let us see
> That which you were meant to be.
> When you are what you'll become,
> Chase the wicked werewolves from
> This, the kingdom we love so.
> Do not tarry, don't be slow.

While saying the last few words, Grassina tossed the tooth outside the ring of fire and waited. The tooth landed behind a patch of ferns so at first they couldn't see it. Then the plants began to shake, twitching violently as an oversized manlike head appeared. Covered with a great mane of tawny hair, the creature opened his mouth wide, showing three rows of teeth, identical to the one from which a golden chain still dangled.

As a tawny back arched above the ferns, a musky smell reached Haywood and Grassina. A trencher-sized paw crushed the plants flat, cracking a branch beside them with a sharp report. When the beast shook himself, a tail tipped with a dense ball of bone and fur twitched, thudding as it hit the ground. Turning to face the werewolves, the horse-sized beast roared, sounding more like a trumpet than a living creature.

"That's a manticore. I've seen drawings of them, but never the real thing," Haywood whispered to Grassina. "He's magnificent!"

"I don't care what he is as long as he gets rid of the werewolves," Grassina replied.

Pippa peeked out of Grassina's sleeve. "How will you get rid of the manticore once he'ss chassed away the werewolvess?"

Grassina bit her lip. "That's a good question."

"I could bite him if you need me to," offered the little snake.

"Thanks," said Grassina, "but I hope that won't be necessary."

Having heard the manticore, the werewolves turned to face this newest threat. When they growled deep in their throats, Haywood put his arm around Grassina and drew her closer to his side. Walking stiff-legged, the werewolves approached the rocks, the fur bristling along their spines. The manticore crouched down, his tail twitching behind him as he eyed the closest werewolf. Suddenly, the beast leapt from atop the rocks, snatched the werewolf in his jaws, tossed it into the air, and caught it on the way down. The werewolf struggled to free itself and actually succeeded for a moment. Then the manticore pounced on it again, batted it with a paw, and let it go just to knock it down again.

"The manticore is playing with the werewolf the way a cat does a mouse," Grassina whispered to Haywood.

He nodded. "It seems we got what we wanted. Those monsters don't stand a chance."

When the werewolf no longer responded, the manticore bit off its head with a horrifying crunch and flung the body aside like a broken toy. Another werewolf approached from behind, so the manticore swung his tail, crushing the creature's skull with one blow of the ball. The carcass hadn't even hit the ground before the rest of the pack turned tail and ran as fast as they could with the manticore close on their heels.

Grassina shuddered and looked away. "I should have

used my spear on them. At least then they'd be turned back into humans and not . . . not . . ."

"Eaten?" said Haywood. "Except you never could have turned them all back. One of them would have gotten to you first, and then you would have been missing a few vital organs."

"Maybe, but what that monster just did makes me sick to my stomach."

"What do you have in mind now?" asked Haywood.

"We'll go to the castle and tell them what happened. Will you go with me?"

"As far as the gates, but I'm not going inside," Haywood said. "I don't think this is the right time to meet your family."

Hand in hand, they started toward the castle, studying the field around them with wary eyes. "Do you see that?" Haywood said suddenly. "There, by those trees. It looks like . . . Yes, I think it is. The manticore is back!"

As the manticore bounded across the farmer's field, Grassina turned to face the beast, gripping her spear firmly. "I wish I knew what he wanted."

"Whatever it is, it can't be good," said Haywood. "Manticores aren't known for being overly friendly."

The manticore stopped only a dozen yards from them and crouched, his wicked-looking tail flicking across his back like an angry pendulum. "You got what you wanted," growled the beast. "I killed a few and scared off the rest." He took a step closer, his shaggy head weaving from side to side. "They won't be back as long as they can smell my scent, which is why you won't kill *me*." Another step and the beast seemed impossibly huge. "If you did, you'd have to face the werewolves all over again."

As the manticore continued his approach, Grassina backed away, uncertain if she should throw her spear or not. One more step and his eyes were boring into hers. "You said I should be quick. Was I too fast for you? I got back before you could run away. I'm sure that wasn't part of your plan. I'm sure this wasn't either."

In a fraction of a second, the manticore rushed at Grassina, knocked the spear from her hand, and swatted her so that she flew into the air. It happened so fast that all she had time to think about was that she was going to die. She didn't realize that she was screaming until her throat hurt. Closing her eyes, she expected to hit the ground hard, but suddenly something soft and fluttery enfolded her in its embrace. Her eyelids flew open. A cloud of moths had surrounded her, breaking her fall. "Haywood!" she breathed as the moths laid her on the ground, then scattered into the night.

Although Grassina was on her feet in an instant, the manticore was already there. This time when the beast batted at her, a flock of owls caught her clothes in their talons and lowered her gently to the farmer's field. She had no intention of playing the manticore's game of cat and mouse, so when the beast pounced on her and rolled her over with its paw, she shouted, "Now, Pippa, bite him!"

Growling deep in his throat, the manticore pinned her to the ground with his paws, letting his decay-scented breath wash over her. Up close, his shaggy head was even bigger than she'd thought; it was at least three times the size of hers, with a mouth large enough to swallow her head and shoulders in one bite. The monster's drool was running into Grassina's ear when Pippa slithered out of her sleeve. Winding herself around the manticore's leg, the snake latched on with her fangs.

A strange look came into the beast's too-human eyes. As the little snake's venom coursed through the monster's veins, the manticore swayed and shook his head. His pupils were dilated, and his breathing was shallow when he slumped toward Grassina. Certain the creature was collapsing just like the werewolf had when Pippa bit it, Grassina tried to squirm out from under him. Instead of crushing her, however, the manticore shook his head again as if he had just awakened from a deep sleep, blinked, and said, "My! I feel so relaxed!"

"Uh oh," said Pippa. "That wass *not* ssuppossed to happen!"

Grassina tried not to flinch when the manticore smiled down at her, grinning so broadly that it looked as if his face might split in two. "I did what you wanted," he said. "Now I'm going to do what *I* want. You never said that I couldn't eat you."

"I wish you—" began Grassina.

"Uh, uh, uh," said the manticore, covering her mouth with his paw. "No magic spells out of you, witch!"

"Hey, monster, over here!" shouted Haywood.

The beast's great head swung toward the young wizard, his eyes narrowed to glittering slits. "Wait your turn. I'll get to you next."

Grassina struggled to breathe, but the manticore's huge paw covered her mouth and her nose. She was writhing under the weight, desperate to break free, when Pippa sank her fangs into the manticore's leg, but without enough time to replenish her venom, her bites had little effect.

Then Haywood shouted, and a moment later the manticore screamed. When he suddenly lifted his paw from her mouth, Grassina gasped for air.

"Ow!" exclaimed the manticore. "Those things can bite! Ow! That hurts!" Plopping down on his haunches, the manticore kicked at his head with his hind foot, then began twisting and thrashing as he snapped at his sides.

"Run!" Pippa said into Grassina's ear, sliding beneath the neck of her tunic.

The beast was rolling on the ground whining when Grassina scrambled out of the way and turned to look. Fire ants were streaming across the monster's fur, biting as they went.

"Quick, over here!" said Haywood, taking her hand. Riddled with crevices, the boulders offered more shelter than anything else they could reach. As they ran, Haywood used his magic to call a bat to lead them to a hiding place. They followed the little creature, climbing over the boulders while the manticore continued to rage. The opening the bat had found was awkwardly placed halfway up the pile of boulders, and almost too narrow for Haywood's shoulders. He squirmed in first, then helped Grassina wriggle through. The manticore had followed them and was sniffing at the bottom of the pile as Grassina pulled her feet in after her.

"Do you have anything elsse in that bag that could help?" asked Pippa.

Grassina shook her head. "That was all I had. I can try to think of a spell, but I'm not very good at it."

"Ah!" said the manticore from outside their hole. "Here you are!"

Grassina lurched backward when the manticore's paw reached inside to grope the air only inches away from her. "I know you're in there! Do you honestly think a few rocks are going to stop me?"

"About that spell . . . ," said Haywood.

A grinding sound made them scoot as far from the opening as they could manage. The manticore was moving the boulders, trying to force his way inside. "I can't think when he's doing that!" said Grassina.

Haywood sat back and placed the wooden box on his lap. "Then I guess it's up to me. I was hoping I'd never have to try this, but I don't have any choice. What I'm about to do is very dangerous, so don't come any closer."

Grassina held her breath while Haywood muttered a spell and removed the lid of the wooden box. For the first time she could see what was inside. A bed of hot coals filled the box, and on the bed slept a small red lizard, glowing even brighter than the smoldering coals.

"Who is that?" asked Pippa.

"*What* is that?" asked Grassina.

"It's a red salamander," said Haywood. "I was learning how to handle it when I started the fire in my father's stable. Red salamanders know more about fire than any other creature, besides dragons, that is, but they are very hard to control."

"You've had that with you all this time and never told me? Oh!" she gasped. "Is that what made those burn marks in the swamp? And I thought it was a dragon! But that salamander is so little. What can it do against a monster like the manticore?"

"You'll see," said Haywood. "I have a spell I can try. . . . I just hope it works."

> Little salamander friend,
> Take your flames and with them wend
> 'Round the manticore so dire

To protect us with your fire.
Make a wall to force him back
And forestall his next attack.

When Haywood held up the box, the salamander took a burning coal in its mouth and scurried out the opening of the shelter. Once out of the box, the little creature shed crackling flames wherever it went. Smoke wafted back into the hole where Grassina and Haywood had taken refuge, making them cough and rub their eyes.

The manticore bellowed close enough to the hole that the rocks around them shook, and Grassina feared that they would be buried alive. Frightened, Pippa wrapped herself around her wrist so tightly that Grassina's hand began to turn blue.

The commotion outside continued, then suddenly grew fainter, and the rocks around them stilled.

"Thank goodness!" said Grassina. "I'm glad you thought of that salamander spell. I didn't know that small magic could make such a difference. I guess it depends on how you use it."

"That's true of any magic," said Haywood. "Have you come up with your spell yet? The salamander won't get rid of the manticore, just hold him off for a while."

"I think I'm ready," said Grassina. "But I want to see him when I say the spell to make sure it actually works."

"I'll go firsst." Unwinding her body from Grassina's

wrist, Pippa slithered out the opening. "That manticore almosst got in. He moved a lot of rockss. You can come out now. He'ss too bussy to notice you."

Getting out of the shelter was easier than getting in had been; the manticore had moved most of the smaller rocks out of the way. Grassina crawled out on her hands and knees, saying, "Haywood, I'm glad you had that box with you to . . . Oh, my!" She had spotted the manticore.

It had run about a hundred feet from the rock pile before the salamander had trapped it. A wall of flame rose up around the manticore; each time the beast tried to leap over the fire, the flames shot higher, singeing its fur and making it fall back, bellowing.

"This is close enough," Haywood said as he got to his feet behind her.

Grassina nodded. "I think so, too." Raising her arm, she pointed at the manticore and said,

> Fierce and nasty you may be,
> But you will not frighten me.
> Though you're big and though you're strong,
> You won't stay that way for long.
> Shrink in strength and shrink in size
> Till you wear a kitten's guise.
> Let your scent be all that stays
> To remind us of your ways.

The manticore was pacing within his fiery cage when he began to shrink. He was smaller than a newborn lamb when the salamander ran off into the night, letting the flames die away. Having extinguished his fire, the little creature was almost impossible to see in the dark.

"Where's he going?" asked Pippa.

Haywood shrugged. "I don't know. I doubt I'll ever see him again."

"But I will," said Pippa, raising her head to taste the air with her flicking tongue. With her head still raised, she slithered off after the salamander.

Grassina hadn't taken her eyes from the manticore. It had stopped shrinking when it reached the size of a three-week-old kitten, but looked in every other way exactly as it had before. "Why doesn't he look like a kitten?" she asked. "He was supposed to after that spell."

"A manticore's a magical beast," said Haywood. "Our magic doesn't work the same on them."

The manticore tried to bellow, but instead of the blare of a trumpet, it sounded more like the tootle of a flute. Frustrated, the beast ran at Grassina as if to attack her again. When it reached her feet, she clucked her tongue and picked him up by the scruff of his neck. The manticore mewed pitifully when she held him at arm's length. "That's much better," said Grassina.

"What have you done to me?" squealed the kitten-sized beast.

Grassina set the creature on the ground, hardly noticing when he swung his tail and tapped her on the wrist with the ball. "Nothing that you don't deserve," she said. "You were right when you said I didn't want to kill you, but then, I didn't want anyone else to be killed either. Good-bye, little one. You should be happy. You wanted to be free to do whatever you desired, and now you are."

As the manticore darted off into the grass, Haywood once again took Grassina's hand in his. "What's this?" he said.

"Hmm?" said Grassina. Turning back from watching the manticore, she let her eyes follow Haywood's. There was a ring on her finger now, a green ring made of a single stone carved to look like overlapping leaves. "Oh," she breathed and glanced up at Haywood. "Do you know what this means? That's the ring of the Green Witch!"

"Which means that you hold the title now," said Haywood, his words clipped and dry. "I'm so happy for you."

"Isn't it wonderful?" said Grassina. "I have to go tell my family. Greater Greensward has a Green Witch again!"

"It is wonderful," said Haywood, "for the kingdom."

Eighteen

rassina and Haywood had almost reached the castle when they ran into an armored party mounted on horseback. Prince Limelyn was at the head of the column, leading King Aldrid's ten bravest knights. "What are you doing here, Princess?" he said, his armor rattling as he doffed his helmet. "It isn't safe. We've come to do battle with a terrible beast that's been heard in the forest. We'll escort you back to—"

"That won't be necessary," said Grassina. "It was a manticore, but we've already taken care of it."

Prince Limelyn looked astounded. "Was it you, good sir?" he asked Haywood. "Tell us how you were able to perform such a marvelous deed!"

"I helped, that's all," said Haywood. "Princess Grassina did most of it herself. Look!" he said, holding up Grassina's hand. The green ring glittered on her finger as it caught the morning sun.

"Is that . . . ?"

"It must be!"

"Princess Grassina is the new Green Witch!"

The knights urged their horses forward, forming a circle around Grassina. Removing their helmets, they gazed at her with respect and admiration. Although she tried to keep hold of Haywood's hand, he had seen the expressions on the knights' faces, and it seemed to make him uncomfortable. "Good-bye, my darling," he said, raising Grassina's hand to his lips. "I must go now. You have to tell your family your news. I'm sure there will be work for you to do as well. You don't need me any longer. These gentlemen will see you safely home."

One of the knights struggled to dismount under the weight of his armor. When he finally had his feet on the ground, he stood between Grassina and Haywood. Draping the reins across his horse's neck, he turned to Grassina, saying, "Your Highness, please do me the honor of riding my steed back to the castle."

"Just a minute," she said, trying to look around him. "Haywood! I need to talk to you. Don't go!"

The knight stepped aside, but Haywood had already slipped past the horses. "Your Highness," said the knight. Leading her to his mount, he helped Grassina into the saddle. She could see farther once she was seated—far enough to see Haywood disappear into the morning mist.

Grassina was still thinking about Haywood when the horses clattered across the courtyard to the foot of the stairs. She didn't notice that her mother and sister were waiting in the midst of Chartreuse's suitors until Olivene called out, "Is that you, Grassina? What are you doing with those men?"

"We have excellent news," said Prince Limelyn as his squire helped him dismount. "Princess Grassina wears the ring of the Green Witch on her finger!"

"She can't!" blurted Chartreuse. When all the princes turned to look at her, she added, "I mean, she wasn't wearing it yesterday."

"Let me see!" crowed Olivene. "I know what it looks like better than any of you." Grabbing Grassina's hand, she yanked so hard that she nearly pulled her daughter off the horse. "That's it, all right. Congratulations. You now have the worst job in the kingdom. It's about time someone in this family did a little work around here, besides me, that is."

"Well, I never . . . ," sputtered Chartreuse.

"See, she admits it. She never could do a decent lick of work."

"Mother!" cried Chartreuse, blushing scarlet.

Prince Torrance pushed his way to the front. "Princess Grassina, may I be the first to congratulate you."

"No!" snapped Olivene. "I already did!"

"And I'd like to wish you well," Torrance continued. "I've always considered you remarkably intelligent and beautiful. Being the Green Witch will simply add to your long list of accomplishments."

"I'm going to be ill," muttered Olivene.

"I can't believe my ears!" exclaimed Chartreuse. "Just the other day you told me that you were glad Grassina wasn't around anymore to distract you with her silly prattling!"

Torrance looked irritated when he glanced at Chartreuse. "I'm sure you must have misunderstood me. I would never be so unkind as to say such a thing about dear, sweet Grassina."

"I say," piped up Prince Miguel, "you do sit that horse well, Grassina."

Prince Stephen scowled. "She'll make a good witch. We could use someone like her in my kingdom. Might keep the minor nobles in line."

"What's going on here?" said Chartreuse. "She's still the same person she was the other day when none of you had time for her. And now you're talking to her and ignoring me!" As if someone had opened a sluice gate, tears flowed from Chartreuse's eyes, and her bottom lip quivered. Dabbing at her eyes, she turned her back to her suitors. "I'm sorry. A princess should never cry in public."

Prince Limelyn was at her side in an instant. "Your Highness," he said. Taking her hand in his, he spoke to her in a voice so quiet that only she could hear it.

"Do you mean that?" Chartreuse asked through her

tears. "You want to marry me whether I have magic or not?"

"With all my heart," said the prince.

"What do you intend to do as your first act as the Green Witch?" Torrance asked Grassina.

"Um . . . I . . ."

"More to the point," said Prince Stephen, "have you thought about getting married? I have a lot to offer a wife."

Chartreuse's eyes flashed. "*I* would like to make an announcement. I have chosen the prince who will become my king. He is brave and true," she said, giving Torrance a nasty look, "unlike some others I could mention. I have decided to marry Prince Limelyn."

"Good for you," said Prince Miguel. "Grassina, you haven't answered Stephen's question. Have you thought about marriage?"

"You're not too young," said Torrance. "If anything, Chartreuse is a bit on the old side."

"Do you mean it, Chartreuse?" Limelyn asked, cupping her face in his hands. "Do you really want to marry me?"

"Yes," she replied. "It would make me the happiest woman in the kingdom. There is no one with whom I'd rather spend the rest of my life." Limelyn was drawing her into his arms when Chartreuse whispered to Olivene. "Don't try to talk me out of it, Mother."

Olivene snorted. "Why would I? You can marry whomever you wish. After all, *you* aren't the Green Witch."

Limelyn had already wrapped his arms around Chartreuse, and so didn't see the stricken look on her face.

"Come, Grassina, we're all waiting to hear your answer," said Stephen. "Because if you're not interested in getting married, I might as well go home. I've already wasted too much time here as it is."

"As a matter of fact," said Grassina, "I do intend to marry, and I know exactly who my husband will be."

"Good!" said Torrance. "Which one of us is it?"

All three princes crowded closer as if expecting to hear their own names.

"None of you. I met him while I was away. He's kind, thoughtful, and brave. He loves me for me, not for my title or for what I can do for him. He's the perfect man for me," she said, turning to Olivene. "Mother, I know you'll love him as much as I do. He has magic, too!"

"Really?" said Olivene, arching her eyebrows.

"Then I'm leaving!" announced Prince Stephen as he shoved past everyone else on the steps. "Stable boy, saddle my horse!"

"I might as well go, too," said Torrance. "I've heard there's a princess in North Aridia who isn't half bad."

"Care for some company?" asked Miguel. "They're said to have excellent horseflesh in North Aridia. Even the women are accomplished riders."

"Congratulations, Grassina," said Limelyn. "When will I meet this lucky fellow?"

"You already have," said Grassina. "Now I just have to let *him* know how lucky he is!"

After visiting her father to share the good news, Grassina hurried back to the swamp. She didn't see Haywood at first, but the fire was burning in the circle of rocks, so she knew he had to be close by. When she sat down to wait for him, she found Pippa stretched out on the rocks beside the fire.

"Pippa, how did you get here so quickly? I thought you were looking for the salamander."

"I found him! Princesss Grasssina, I want you to meet my friend, Igniss."

The fire flamed higher, and something shifted in its depths. Grassina glanced down and was surprised to see the salamander resting comfortably among the glowing embers. "It's nice to meet you, Princess. Pippa has told me all about you," the salamander said in a husky voice.

"It's nice to meet you, too," Grassina replied.

"The moment I saw Iggie, I knew we were meant to be friendss," said Pippa. "He'ss warm and friendly and warm and honesst and. . . . Did I mention how warm he iss? With him around, I'll never be cold again. You were right about my luck. I musst be the luckiesst ssnake in the world to have found a good friend like Iggy, and it wouldn't have happened if Haywood hadn't ssaid hiss ssalamander sspell! It'ss amazing what ssmall magic can do."

"I've been thinking about it, and I don't believe we should call any magic small; certainly nothing Haywood does. He is quite wonderful. Do you know—"

"After I found Iggie, I perssuaded him to come with me," said Pippa. "I told him that I knew of a nice ssafe place where he could live. We were on our way here when we ssaw Haywood and he gave uss a ride."

"Where is Haywood now?" asked Grassina.

"I'm right here," said Haywood, rounding the hut. His eyes brightened when he saw her, but then he shook his head and turned away, although not before Grassina saw his eyes cloud over with despair.

"I was wondering if you'd come to say good-bye," he said.

Grassina shrugged. "I had to come. We have too much left to say."

"No, we don't," said Haywood, turning back to her. "You don't have to explain anything to me. I saw how those men looked at you. You told me about your sister's suitors. I'm sure that you'll have even more now that everyone knows you're the Green Witch. You'll marry a prince, not someone as lowly as me. I'm not worthy of you. I have nothing to offer other than a hut in a swamp. Please, be kind and make this quick. Seeing you is hard enough."

"I don't know why," said Grassina. "Hearing that someone loves you to distraction and wants to marry you shouldn't be all that difficult. Why, when I told the princes back at the castle that I'd already chosen the man I wanted to marry—"

"You want to what?" Haywood asked, blinking at her in confusion.

"Marry you, of course. I've never met anyone who suited me better. Since I couldn't possibly live without you, there's no need to talk of anyone being unworthy. Those princes couldn't hold a candle to you. And I'm the Green Witch now, which means that I can live anywhere in the kingdom and no one can tell me what I can or can't do. Greater Greensward needs me too much. Chartreuse won't dare try to order me around. She's getting married, too, you know. To Prince Limelyn, the only one of the lot whom I could stand."

Haywood pulled her into his arms and kissed her. Wrapping her arms around his waist, Grassina kissed him back and sighed when it was over. She was thinking about how happy she was when Haywood pressed his cheek against the top of her head and said, "But what will your family say? Your mother—"

"My mother will love you. I'm sure of it. And if she doesn't, what can she do? The Green Witch is always the most powerful as well as the nicest witch in the kingdom. No one will dare get between you and me. Just wait and see. Everything will be wonderful. You and I are about to find out what it really means to live happily ever after!"